COPYRIGHT

REVIEWS

He Completes Me by Cardeno C.: With He Completes Me, Cardeno C takes angst out of the equation and gives readers a story worthy of fairytale status. The outcast, black sheep of the family meets and falls in love with the white knight and in turn becomes a hero himself. It would be very poetic if not for Zach. He would say screw the poetry and find some vodka.

— *Joyfully Jay*

Just What the Truth Is by Cardeno C.: Cardeno has laid out a beautifully realistic book of one man's journey to a happy fulfilled life, and the pitfalls he encountered or put up himself that had to be overcome before he could achieve his goals. As I said I loved this book and I think you will too. Don't pass it up.

— *Scattered Thoughts and Rogue Words*

Love at First Sight by Cardeno C.: There wasn't anything that I didn't love about this book. ...I feel as if I'm right there immersed within the story. Watching David and Jonathan fall in love was intense and amazing. Seeing what happened after ... just reinforced my belief that there are good, decent people in the world who know how to love through thick and thin.

— *Rainbow Book Reviews*

The One Who Saves Me by Cardeno C.: Positively phenomenal! A unique spin on the friends to lover theme with an amazing relationship-based story. ...I loved both of these very well developed characters. ... If you enjoy an amazing friends to lovers with benefits theme with great dialogue, strong characters, and an interesting life journey, this more than fits the bill.

— The Romance Reviews

Walk With Me by Cardeno C.: Walk with Me isn't all seriousness and emotion. It's actually quite funny! The dialogue between Eli and Seth is like what you find between happy, fun loving friends. ... It's an emotional journey with Seth and Eli but also one for readers of the Home Series as we celebrate love and commitment but also say goodbye to Emile City.

— 3 Chicks After Dark

Where He Ends and I Begin by Cardeno C.: This was an incredibly sweet romantic story. It's one of those stories where you can believe that the two men will be together from the cradle to the grave and possibly beyond... I would definitely recommend this author and this book to anyone who loves a good romance. It makes you believe that each of us has that one person who completes us.

— The Romance Studio

DEDICATION

To Rachel G., who loves Noah best..

CHAPTER ONE

Noah—Present

A PERSISTENT, annoying sound kept infiltrating my mind. I'd manage to shut it out successfully for a while, only to have it edge its way back in.

"Beep-beep-beep."

What is that noise? Maybe I can find it and make it stop. Ugh—that'll require opening my eyes and my eyelids feel so heavy. I don't think they've ever felt this heavy.

The beep-beep-beep got louder, or maybe I was just more aware of it. And something smelled strange. Not dirty, but not pleasant either. Like a deep, chemical smell.

"Beep-beep-beep."

What is that? Did we get a new alarm clock? We've never needed one. Clark's body has the amazing ability to know what time it is even when he's asleep, so he hasn't ever let us sleep too late.

"Beep-beep-beep."

Maybe I can reach it and make it stop. Don't need to open my eyes for that, just need to lift my arm. Oh, that feels heavy too.

And it aches. Why does my arm ache? It's not just my arm; my legs hurt too, both of them. And my chest feels so tight, almost like it's burning. What in the hell is going on?

Clark. I need Clark. He'll make it better.

I tried to call out to him, but my tongue felt thick and heavy and my mouth felt like it was full of cotton. I forced myself to concentrate every ounce of energy I had on my tongue, my mouth. If I could get just one word out, it'd all be better. He'd make it better.

"Clark?"

My voice sounded weak and broken, completely foreign to my ears.

"Oh my God, Noah. Noah? Can you hear me? Are you awake?"

Pain and exhaustion turned into anger in the blink of an eye. *That is, if I could blink my eye, which I can't, because blinking requires opening and opening requires eye strength that I apparently don't have. Wait, I can lift twice my body weight and I just complained about the strength of my eyelids? Seriously?* Anyway, the point is that wasn't Clark's voice. Well, the plus side of anger is adrenaline, and that gave me strength for more words.

"What did you do, Ben? Where's Clark? What did you do to Clark?"

As my brain began to clear, panic gripped me. Deep, breath-stealing, heart-pounding, sweat-inducing panic. I couldn't move my body, couldn't open my eyes, and my lover wasn't there. It was the last one that really terrified me.

"If you hurt him, Ben...I swear I'll kill you. What in the hell did you do to Clark?"

My voice sounded stronger and the beeping noise was louder, or maybe faster, I wasn't sure. With significant effort, I finally managed to pry my eyes open.

A dull, grayish shade of white. Everything. The walls, the acoustic tile ceilings, the fluorescent lights, the sheets, they were all a dingy white color.

Where in the hell am I? Television anchored to the wall, a metal tray beneath it, and a door next to that. Coarse, heavy, white sheets covered me. Oh, and don't forget the beeping. The ever-present beeping.

"I didn't do anything. You were in an accident, Noah. You've been out for weeks. I've been so worried. Thank goodness you're finally awake."

He grasped my hand and I willed my eyes to focus on my brother's face. His normally perfect hair was messy, his shirt wrinkled, and his eyes wet with unshed tears. All of those things were unusual for my brother, but what I noticed most of all was that he looked older, not just a so-tired-that-his-face-looks-haggard type of older, though that was there too. But it was more than that. His movie-star face looked years older.

It had been two years since I'd last seen my brother, which would make him, what? Twenty-eight next month, just a couple of months younger than Clark. Did he really age that much in two years? Wait, did he say weeks? I blinked my eyes and made myself focus on what mattered.

"Where is Clark?"

My brother looked anxious and surprised.

"Damn it, Ben! Answer me! What's wrong with him? Where is he? Was he in the accident? I want to see him. I *need* to see him. Where is Clark?"

The panic was almost blinding. I couldn't breathe. Then everything started going black.

There's no way Clark would leave me alone in a hospital unless he was... No.

I wouldn't even let myself finish that thought. The beeping was closer together, incessant, almost like one long sound with no separation.

"What's going on in here? Oh! He's awake. I'll page the doctor."

A portly woman in pink scrubs pushed her way past my brother, reached above my head, and turned a dial on a machine next to me, successfully managing to stop that god-awful beeping noise. Halle-fricken-lujah.

"Mr. Forman? Can you hear me?"

I closed my eyes, forced myself to breath more slowly, then focused on the nurse.

"Of course I can hear you. Please, can you tell me where my partner is? Clark Lehman. Is he a patient here? Is he okay? I need to see him. Please."

She looked confused, opened her mouth to answer,

and then…

"Mr. Forman. It's wonderful to see you awake. I'm Dr. Garcia."

A dark-haired man in charcoal dress slacks, a blue button-down shirt, and a white lab coat took a penlight from his pocket and shined it in my eyes.

"Can you follow this light, Mr. Forman?"

The light moved from side to side. I humored him for about five seconds, before I went back to my question.

"Dr…."

"Garcia. Dr. Garcia."

"Right. Listen, Dr. Garcia, I'll be happy to follow your light or whatever, but first I need someone to tell me where my partner is. I'm starting to freak out here, man. His name is Clark Lehman. He should be here. I know he'd be here if he could. I need to know if something happened to Clark."

I felt the tears building up behind my eyes. He couldn't be. Not possible. I'd know it if he was.

"Is he…"

I swallowed and forced myself to continue.

"Is he…is Clark dead?"

Even saying the words hurt. An all-consuming, can't-feel-anything-else, see-no-reason-to-go-on-living kind of hurt. I closed my eyes to ease the pain and fell back into the darkness.

Clark—Past

BENJAMIN FORMAN was over six feet tall, with broad shoulders, a narrow waist, and bulging muscles. He had thick, chestnut hair that always seemed to lie on his head in a perfect style with every hair in place, big, wide-set brown eyes that twinkled when he laughed, full red lips, a straight nose, strong jaw, and a perfect symmetry to his handsome face that any model would have envied. He was on the starting lineups of our high school basketball, baseball, and football teams. He was in student council, honors classes, and he volunteered two afternoons a week to tutor the English as a Second Language students. He was voted homecoming king, prom king, best-looking, and most likely to succeed our senior year. And, in addition to all of those other things, he was my best friend.

There I was, the new kid in town, spending lots of time with Mister You're-too-perfect-to-be-real. This should be the part of the story where I tell you that I had a crush on Ben. And, in a real fantasy tale, I'd say that, after months or even years of angst and trauma, he admitted that he was madly, deeply in love with me. But that wasn't the case. Ben was into girls and I had never had any feelings other than platonic friendship for the guy. He simply wasn't my type. His brother, on the other hand, captivated me from the moment I saw him. Noah Forman was my everything from day one.

Trying to describe Noah is like trying to describe

the wind during a rainstorm. You can smell it and feel it all around you, even if you can't see it. Sometimes the wind is so palpable that you can literally taste it, without so much as opening your mouth. And, if it's a big storm, the wind can feel wild and chaotic, as if it's coming at you from all directions. That's Noah. Not that you can't see him, of course. The man isn't invisible. It's just that his essence is so powerful you don't need your eyes to see him. At least I never had—my reaction to him had always been visceral and all-encompassing.

I know that describing someone as wild, chaotic, and coming at you from all directions might sound like a person who bounces from thing to thing, someone without direction or commitment. But that's not Noah, not one bit. He somehow manages to merge wild and free with dedicated and sure. And he has always been committed to me, from the first time I met him, when I was seventeen and Noah was thirteen.

MY MOTHER and I had moved to Emile City that year to live close to my aunt and uncle, so they could take care of me if my mom died before I turned eighteen. Oh yeah, did I mention I was starting to lose my best friend that year? I haven't switched topics; my mom was my best friend. And I was hers.

I had never known my father, which wasn't a Greek tragedy or anything. My mom and I were super-tight. It had always been just the two of us. I didn't think about my father much, but when I did ask about him, my mom was always complimentary. She said he was a nice man, serious, smart, and handsome, with blue eyes like mine. They hadn't known each other long before she got pregnant. And by the time she'd realized I was on the way, they'd already moved on from each other. It was amicable, like all the endings to my mother's relationships. Nobody could ever stay angry at my mother.

She'd thought about telling him he was going to be a father, but he'd already left town by then, off to greener pastures, and he'd always said he wasn't interested in having kids or getting married. So she figured there was no reason to upset his life. She was forty years old, had a good job as an art curator, and she'd always wanted a baby. So she'd decided to keep me. In her mind, I was her responsibility, not his.

She'd never stopped me from looking him up, never made me feel like I'd be betraying her or anything. I just hadn't been interested. I thought maybe someday I'd do it so I could see what he looked like, let him know that he had a kid out there in the world. But that day hadn't come when my mother was diagnosed with ovarian cancer. By the time the doctors discovered it, there wasn't much anyone could do for her other than hold her hand through aggressive chemotherapy and hope that she'd be one of the few people who survived the disease.

My mom was tiny, barely five feet tall and maybe eighty-five pounds. Having inherited my father's height, along with his eyes, I was already taller and broader than her at the age of sixteen. The day she told me about her diagnosis, we sat together on the purple faux-suede couch of our little beach house and I held her in my arms while we cried. When we ran out of tears and tissues, she said that we'd have to move. She wanted to be somewhere I could stay if the worst happened and she didn't make it.

That was my mom, always a straight shooter. She didn't sugarcoat anything or treat me like a kid. We both knew her chances of survival were slim and she wasn't going to insult my intelligence by pretending otherwise. I loved and appreciated that about her, even though a part of me wanted to bury my head in the sand and pretend she wasn't sick, wasn't dying, and wasn't going to leave me all alone in the world.

So that day on the couch, my mom gave me the option of finding my father or going with her to live close to her sister in Emile City. Because seeing my father held no real interest for me, I chose the latter, not knowing that I would truly find my home there. And I'm not talking about my aunt and uncle's house. I'm talking about Noah.

I STARTED school halfway through the year, but caught up fast. Schoolwork wasn't particularly difficult for me, and I did well socially. I joined the baseball team as soon as the season started, knowing that it'd be a good way to make friends. I wasn't a great athlete, but I wasn't terrible either. Basically, I did well enough to get on the team and not embarrass myself.

Ben Forman was the best player on the team. He probably would have been captain, except the coaches saved that privilege for a senior. So Ben and I played baseball together, and because we were both juniors, we had a few classes together. Then one day at lunch, Ben called me over to sit with him and some other guys, which became my lunchtime routine. And that was how he became the next breadcrumb on the trail that led me home, led me to Noah.

It all started like an average Friday. I had no idea that my life was about to change. Hell, change was an understatement—my life was going to look up; it was going to explode; it was going to *start*.

Ben had invited a few of us from the team to sleep over at his house after the game that night. I'd heard from the other guys that Ben had stopped having people over to his house a couple of years prior, so they were pretty excited about the invite. I'd almost turned him down because I'd been worried about leaving my mom, but she'd insisted.

"A night away from here will do you some good, honey. Don't worry about missing any excitement, I'll count the number of times I throw up during the night and fill you in when you get back tomorrow."

The fact that she could even make jokes while her body was falling apart right before our eyes was a testament to my mother's strength and good nature.

"Are you sure? You know I don't mind being here if you need me."

We were living in a small, two-bedroom apartment that was walking distance from my aunt and uncle's place. I had my own room, but I'd been sleeping with my mom since we'd gotten there. That way, I could get her whatever she needed during the night, and help her walk to the bathroom when she got nauseous, which was almost constantly.

She pushed herself up with her shaky hands, lifting up from her bed, and patted my cheek.

"Of course I need you, sweet boy. You're my whole world. But I have all of my medicine here, the home health nurse will be by at five o'clock, and I'll probably be sleeping most of the time anyway. I'll be fine."

I gave her a gentle hug. She was all skin and bones, so I was constantly worried I'd break her if I squeezed too tight.

"I'm sorry that I can't come see your games, honey. You know I wish I could."

I kissed her forehead and held back the tears. Her skin felt so cold and clammy.

"It's no big deal. I'm sure I'll just be warming the bench the whole game."

Okay, that wasn't true. I wasn't a great player, but I was good enough for starting rotation. And I wasn't in the habit of lying to my mom, but I didn't want her to feel bad about missing my games. I knew she'd be there if she could.

CHAPTER TWO

Noah—Present

I FOUGHT my way through the darkness and heard my brother's voice. He was angry, almost yelling. It took several seconds for me to remember what had happened—I was in the hospital and Clark wasn't there. Clark. I needed Clark.

"I will not call him!"

"Please, Ben. Your brother isn't out of the woods yet. A car accident like that, most people wouldn't have survived. His size and strength got him this far, but his body is recovering and he can't handle any extra stress and tension. You saw how upset he was. He literally passed out because of it, and I don't know when or if he'll wake back up. He asked for his partner, and from what Nurse Smith told me, he did the same thing when she came into the room and she heard him asking you. How is it that you don't understand how tenuous this situation is, Ben?"

"You're the one who doesn't understand. We can't call Clark Lehman. He's..."

Oh, he did not just say that. Did Ben really just refuse to call Clark? Seriously?

"Get out."

Hello, voice. Welcome back.

My brother and Dr. Garcia turned to me, clearly surprised to hear me speaking. I managed to make my left arm work enough to push up on the bed so that I could raise my body to something resembling a sitting position.

"You heard me, Ben. Get out of here."

He came over to me, pain filling his eyes.

"Noah, listen to me..."

I turned to the doctor.

"He doesn't have the right to be here, and he doesn't have the right to keep my partner away."

I glared at my brother without trying to hide the anger and hate I was feeling at that moment.

"We're gay, not stupid, Ben, despite what you might think."

I was seething, wanting to crush his damn windpipe for coming between me and my lover. I wiggled my fingers and sighed in frustration, when I realized I didn't have the strength. Oh well, I'd have to settle for ignoring that piece of shit. I looked at the doctor.

"My physician's name is Dr. James Reed. He has a copy of my healthcare power of attorney. Please call him and then call my partner. I'm estranged from my family, Dr. Garcia, so I don't want them here. Especially him."

I gestured to my brother with my head but refused

to meet his stare. The doctor looked at my brother with sad eyes.

"Don't feel sorry for him, Dr. Garcia. I don't know what he told you while I was out, but it's been more than two years since my brother has spoken to me or to the man who thought he was his best friend. Ask him why, Dr. Garcia. Or can you guess?"

"Noah, please."

Ben stepped closer to me. I clenched my jaw and spoke through gritted teeth.

"Oh, I see. You're not in the mood for guessing games. Is that it, Ben? Or is it that you don't want me to expose your hateful ass? Listen to me. We've had enough, okay? You aren't going to change who we are and keeping Clark away from me while I'm in the hospital is low, even for you. The only reason you're still standing is because I can't move my body, but that won't last forever, so do yourself a favor and get out!"

The doctor rushed over to me and put his hand on my shoulder.

"Noah, please calm down. I'll call your partner, okay? Clark Lehman? That's what you said, right? You're smart to have legal papers, Noah, but as long as you're awake, we won't need them. You can make your own decisions, including who can visit you. So just stay with us, okay?"

I nodded and let my body relax. Clark wasn't dead; my homophobic brother had been keeping him away. We hadn't spent a single night apart for almost six years. We couldn't sleep without each other and didn't want to. My brother said I'd been in that hospital for weeks, which meant he'd been keeping Clark away from me for that long.

At least I'd had the good fortune to be unconscious the entire time. I didn't even want to think about what Clark must have been going through, knowing I was hurt and hospitalized yet being kept away. He was probably miserable; hopefully, seeing that I was fine would make him feel better.

Clark—Past

WE WON the game that night, so everyone was in a great mood when we got to Ben's place. We traipsed into the family room, watched videos, played games, ate junk food, and wrestled on the floor. At midnight, Mrs. Forman came in and told us it was time to hit the sack.

"One of us will have to crash in my brother's room tonight. I only have the extra bunk and the trundle in my room."

The other two guys groaned and Ben rolled his eyes knowingly. Clearly, there was a story there and I was curious about it, but his mother had said it was time to go to bed and

I wasn't one to disobey a mother. Even someone else's.

"I'll sleep in your brother's room, dude."

I picked up my backpack from where I'd dropped it behind the couch when we'd gotten there.

"Point the way."

Ben snickered, got off the floor, walked over to me, and patted my back.

"Brave man. His room is down that hallway, last door on the right. There's an attached bathroom."

I'd seen neither hide nor hair of Ben's brother in the two and a half hours we'd been in that house, so I wasn't sure whether he was home. I slung my backpack over my shoulder and turned to Ben.

"Is he asleep? Should I be quiet?"

More laughter from the other two guys. Ben just shrugged.

"Who knows? He can be sort of...unpredictable and loud, so my folks closed in the third garage bay last year and used lots of insulation. That way his room is far enough away from the rest of us that we don't have to hear his, ehm, noise."

I started to get nervous. I shifted from foot to foot and chewed on my bottom lip.

"What kind of noise?"

Jim and Pete, the other two guys from the team, exchanged looks then jumped into the conversation.

"Man, Ben's brother is a total freak. I heard that last year he—"

Pete didn't get to finish his sentence because Ben turned on him and growled.

"Hey, shut the fuck up. He's my *brother*, asshole."

I decided to let it drop. Ben was right; we had no place bad-talking his brother. Besides, there was no noise anyone could make that would be worse than listening to my mother cry during her sleep, and I'd been living with that for months.

"Last door on the right. Got it. See you pricks in the a.m."

I made kissy faces in the air, which caused Ben to laugh and consequently lightened the mood. I had a smile on my face as I walked down the hall and thought about how protective Ben was of his brother. It was one of those things where he could say whatever he wanted about the guy, but no one else had better say a word. That was exactly how things should be. After all, family was family. Being someone who was about to lose the only real family I had, I understood that better than anyone.

When I reached the last door in the hallway, I knocked gently, not wanting to wake Ben's brother if he was already asleep. No answer. I cracked the door open and poked my head in.

There were two twin beds in the room and the moonlight streaming in through the window was enough for me to see that both were empty. I figured maybe he was in the bathroom and I didn't want to startle him when he came out, so I dropped my backpack on the bed closest to me and knocked on the bathroom door.

"Hello? I'm Ben's friend, Clark Lehman. I'm going to be bunking in your room tonight."

Nothing. Not a sound. And I noticed there wasn't any light coming out from under the door. Hmmm. Guess Ben's brother was out for the night. I figured he was probably sleeping over at a friend's house and Ben didn't know about it. I hit the switch for the ceiling light and looked around the room.

The floor was stained concrete, unlike the wall-to-wall carpeting and wood floors in the rest of the house. The walls and ceiling were painted with a mishmash of crayons, markers, and paint. On top of that, there were layers of band posters. Groups I didn't listen to—Rob Zombie, the Butthole Surfers, Social Distortion, the Dead Milkmen, and the Cure. The furniture seemed to have suffered a fate similar to the walls—an amateur paint job and lots of band stickers. One of the beds, the one I assumed he slept in, wasn't made, but other than that, the room was neat and orderly.

I got my Dopp kit out of my backpack and went into the attached bathroom. As soon as I turned on the lights, I saw a plain room—white walls, stock cabinets, brown shower curtain. A regular bathroom, but it seemed dull and lifeless in comparison to the vibrant bedroom I'd just stepped out of.

I brushed my teeth, washed my face, and used the toilet. Then I went back into the bedroom, turned off the lights, and stripped down to my boxer briefs. I had just pulled back the comforter on the bed when I heard a scraping noise behind me.

"Who the fuck are you, and what are you doing in my bedroom?"

I turned my head and saw a guy straddling the windowsill, half in and half out of the room. His hair was purple and sticking up all over his head, he had black eyeliner smeared under his eyes, and three rings in the top of his left ear. Black and green polish was chipping off his fingernails. His black shirt was full of holes and his loose jeans, also black, were in similar condition.

He stepped over the windowsill and into the room. I looked at his face and beautiful hazel eyes met my gaze. My breath left me in a sudden whoosh as I realized I was looking at my future. I wasn't able to identify my feelings for him then, and it'd be years before I'd figure them out. But even in that first moment I knew he was my responsibility, mine to take care of, even though I didn't know his name.

I realized that first look shook something in him too, because as soon as our eyes met, his previously angry expression softened. He walked over to me and stood so close I could feel the heat from his skin radiate onto mine. It felt wonderful.

I was taller than him by about six inches, which wasn't unusual, because at over six feet tall, I was taller than most people. Even with his shorter height, his shoulders were just as broad as mine. Again, not a surprise, considering the fact that his brother and his father were both big guys, and I was more tall and lanky.

He reached his hand up and cupped my cheek in an intimate and tender gesture. Instead of pulling away, my body instinctively moved toward his touch. It should have been uncomfortable, but it felt like the most natural thing in the world to press closer to him.

"You look like an angel. What's your name?"

His voice sounded calmer and less threatening than it had when he'd first crawled through the window and discovered me in his room.

"Clark."

He nodded and closed his eyes.

"Clark. Okay, then. I'm Noah, and boy, are you ever the last thing I expected."

I was about to ask him what he meant, when I noticed bruises all over his neck. A protective wave washed over me. I wanted to draw Noah close to my body and keep him safe. Somehow, I held myself back, and instead I touched the marks gently with my fingers, wishing I could heal them and take away his pain.

"Are you okay? What happened to you? Did someone hurt you?"

He seemed confused by my question. I realized I had been touching him for too long, so I dropped my hand. Noah walked into the bathroom, turned on the light, leaned over the counter, and looked into the mirror while pressing on the bruises.

"Huh. Well, my parents are bound to have a shit fit about this tomorrow."

He turned back around and faced me.

"They're hickies. I didn't have them when I went to bed tonight, so my parents are going to realize I snuck out."

He shrugged his shoulders in a silent acknowledgement that he didn't really care what his parents thought.

"Well, maybe that'll teach them a lesson about trying to ground me."

Then he took his shirt off and pushed his pants and briefs to the ground.

"I'm going to take a shower. I hate the smell of cigarette smoke."

I was listening to Noah, trying to process what he was saying and to wrap my brain around this guy who was so different from anyone I'd ever known. But then I was distracted by his dick. No, not in a sexual way. My feelings for him, while undeniably intense, weren't sexual at that time. The reason I was staring at his dick was because it was... colorful.

He noticed the direction of my gaze and looked down at himself. Then he chuckled.

"There was a rainbow room at the party I went to."

"A what?"

"A rainbow room."

I had absolutely no idea what he was talking about. He leaned against the bathroom counter, crossed his arms, and looked at me appraisingly. I thought maybe he was trying to decide if he could trust me and whether I was worth his time. Ultimately, the answer must have been yes, because he kept talking.

"It's a room where guys go to get blow jobs. There's a bowl of lipsticks by the door and you put some on before you suck. Everyone takes turns so that by the time you get off, your dick is covered with lots of different shades."

Shocked would be an understatement to describe what I was feeling. At seventeen, I'd never had a girlfriend, never been kissed, and most certainly never received a blow job. To have him tell me so nonchalantly that this was a party game made me speechless.

Then he took it a step further when he spun around, lifted his chin as he peered into the mirror, wiped his lips with the back of his hand, and looked at it as he moved it back and forth under the light.

"Guess mine's all gone. I was wearing purple."

"What?" I asked, sure I misheard.

He didn't stop the careful examination of his hand.

"Purple. I chose a purple shade because I know it lasts, but it must have rubbed off. Hopefully it was after I was done sucking."

Another shrug, then he turned away from the mirror and walked to the shower. He adjusted the water temperature and stepped in. I was rooted to my spot on the floor in front of the bathroom.

Did Ben's brother just tell me that he went to sex parties, got blow jobs from multiple people, *and* gave them? I shook my head, thinking that I had to be hallucinating.

CHAPTER THREE

Noah—Present

"NOAH? CAN you hear me?"

I groaned and opened my eyes.

"Of course I can hear you, Dr. Garcia. You're standing less than a foot away from my face."

He chuckled and smiled sheepishly.

"Sorry about that, Noah. I was worried that we lost you again."

I nodded in understanding.

"Where's Clark? Did you tell him he can come here? I know he must be worried sick."

The penlight came back, and Dr. Garcia was shining it in my eyes, turning my head from side to side, and looking pretty pleased with himself.

"Yes. The nurse spoke with him. He's on his way here. As long as we're waiting and you're awake, I'd like to ask you a few questions."

I felt so relieved Clark was coming that I was willing to agree to anything.

"Yeah, sure, Doc. Whatever, shoot."

"What's your full name?"

I laughed.

"Wow. Starting with the hard stuff right out of the chute, huh? My name is Noah Asher Forman."

He looked down at the clipboard in his lap and made a note.

"Wonderful. When's your birthday, Noah?"

"October twenty-ninth. Can you guess the theme for most of my birthday parties as a kid? I'll give you a clue—there was lots of black and orange."

Dr. Garcia laughed, made another note on his clipboard, and looked back at me.

"Do you know today's date, Noah?"

"See, now that's a trick question because Ben said I've been here for a few weeks. That isn't exactly a clear period of time."

He nodded.

"Fair enough. How about just telling me the last date you remember, and I'll do the necessary math, seeing as how I know how long you've been in this hospital?"

"December twenty-sixth."

The doctor's eyes snapped to mine and his brow furrowed.

"And...and the year?"

Dr. Garcia's eyes stayed focused on mine and his expression was completely smooth. But the hitch in his voice betrayed his calm exterior.

"There are no wrong answers here, Noah. The complete date, including the year?"

I was getting tired. I leaned back on the pillows and closed my eyes.

"December 26, 2007."

No response. The long silence was eerie. I opened my eyes to Dr. Garcia's worried gaze. He shook his head, blinked, and started writing on his clipboard.

"What's the last thing you—"

"Noah?"

Oh thank Christ! The sound of that warm, caring, velvet voice rolled through me and settled my bones. That familiar, comforting voice was all I needed to relax me. It was all I'd ever needed.

"I'm right here, Clark. I'm fine. I'm sorry Ben kept you away, angel, but it's all right now. He's gone and they know you belong here."

I looked over at the figure coming through the door, my heart rate quickening in anticipation of his touch, his smell, his taste. Six years living together and he still did that to me, always would. My Clark, my angel, *mine.*

As soon as he got close to me, I realized something was off. He didn't look the same. I mean, he looked worried and anxious, which was unusual, but there was more to it. His strawberry-blond hair was lighter and longer than last time I'd seen him, and I knew it didn't grow fast enough to get that way in just a few weeks. His bright blue eyes were the same, but there were a couple of crow's-feet on the sides, which was new. His skin was darker than usual too. He was still pretty fair—my guy doesn't tan—but he definitely had more color than I ever remembered seeing on him in the winter. And he had some extra freckles across the bridge of his nose. My chest tightened with that realization. I loved his freckles. So damn cute.

Wait, why did he look so different and, if I had to choose a word...older? Like Ben had looked older. And I didn't mean a few weeks older. Just how long had I been in that hospital?

Clark must have noticed my distress, because he quickened his pace and came right up to the bed, one hand reaching for my cheek, the other for my chest.

"Noah? Are you okay? Breathe, sweetheart."

Dr. Garcia stood up, looking a little disconcerted.

Damn, I needed to calm down or they'd kick Clark out of the room.

I leaned into Clark's touch against my face, covered his hand with mine, breathed in his comforting, familiar scent, and let the air flow in and out of my lungs as feelings of safety washed over me.

"I'm okay now that you're here, angel. I'm just tired and...and confused. You look different, older, so does Ben."

I closed my eyes, took in a few more breaths, and then looked at my lover.

"How long have I been here, Clark? I don't understand

what's going on."

Clark—Past

"SO HOW long have you known my brother? I don't think I've heard him mention your name. Not that I usually listen to whatever that uptight asshole says, but most of his friends have been hanging around here for years, at least until recently, and I know I'd remember *you.*"

Okay, so not a hallucination. Noah was real and talking to me from behind the shower curtain.

"I, uh, I just met Ben a couple of months ago when I transferred here. I was living in Seattle until then. Do you, um, do you go to our school?"

Honestly, I'd have thought he was out of high school but for the fact he'd mentioned being grounded. I assumed parents didn't do that to kids after they graduated, even if they still lived at home. Not that I had much of a reference. My mother had never punished me, mostly because we didn't have a traditional parent-child relationship, but also because I hadn't ever done anything to warrant a punishment. I respected my mother and figured that if she actually took the time to tell me to do something, it was probably the right thing to do. Besides, my mother was much more the "what do *you* think you should do" type rather than the "my way or the highway" type.

The water turned off. Noah pushed the shower curtain aside and took the towel off the rack. He dried his body, then stepped out of the shower while he rubbed the towel through his wet hair.

"Nice to know my brother loves me enough to talk about me to his friends."

"What? No, he didn't say anything about you."

Noah laughed and hung the towel back up. Then he walked over to the sink, picked up his toothbrush, and squeezed the paste on.

"I was being sarcastic, guy. If he'd said word one about me, you'd have known my name. Word two and you'd know I'm too young to be in high school."

Even though he was shorter than me, I'd assumed Noah was older than me. His room, his taste in music, his look, his attitude, his social scene, all of those things made me think he was older.

"How old are you?"

He spit his toothpaste into the sink, lowered his head under the faucet to get water into his mouth, swished it around and spit it out. Then he wiped his mouth with the back of his hand.

"Thirteen."

My jaw dropped open. He walked past me and into the bedroom, climbed onto his bed, completely naked, and covered himself with his blanket.

"Hey, sorry I freaked you out, guy. You're not going to tell my brother about me sneaking out, are you? Because he'll rat me out to our parents and then I'll have to listen to another safe-sex talk from my mother. I really don't want to deal with that shit again."

I didn't know how to respond. To say I was horrified wouldn't cover it, but it seemed as if Noah's parents had some idea of what he was up to and that wasn't stopping him. So telling them probably wasn't going to do anyone any good. Plus, I didn't want to betray his trust. I felt loyal to Noah, even then.

"I, uh, no. I won't tell."

"Cool. Good night, Clark. I'm glad we met. Something tells me we'll be seeing a lot more of each other."

And with that he turned to his side, punched his pillow a couple of times, and fell asleep. I still hadn't moved from my position by the bathroom door. Eventually, I made my way to the bed, laid down, and tried to fall asleep. All the while, I had only one thing on my mind: how was I going to help Noah? Because what I knew for sure was that he needed help and it was my job to give it to him.

I don't know when I finally managed to fall asleep, but I think it was close to sunrise, based on the change in the light coming in from the window. When I woke up, Noah was gone. I sat up in bed, rubbed the backs of my hands over my eyes, and sighed.

Up all night and no idea of how I could help Noah. I didn't even know what I was helping with, just that something was up with him and that he...needed me.

I climbed out of bed, brushed my teeth, splashed some water on my face, and got dressed. Then I packed my Dopp kit and dirty clothes into my backpack, and made my way out to find Ben. I had to get home to make sure my mom was okay, but first I wanted to thank him and his parents for having me over.

As soon as I walked out of Noah's room, I could hear the yelling. I was too far away to make out the words at first, but as I got closer to the kitchen, I realized that Noah was fighting with his parents.

"By sucking on someone's neck, that's how. Don't tell me you don't know how you get a hickey."

Noah's tone was angry and sarcastic.

"That's not what I'm asking you, Noah Asher Forman. I'm asking how you got the, ehm, marks on your neck, considering the fact that you were grounded last night."

His mother's voice was shaking, but it seemed as if she was trying to keep it together.

"And I've already answered that question, *Mother*, I got the marks while I was getting laid. If it's been so long for you that you can't remember how the process works, then I feel sorry for Dad."

I had almost gotten to the kitchen, where they were sitting, when I heard that last bit. I hated hearing how angry

Noah was. That rage had no place in him.

"That is not an acceptable way to talk to your mother, Noah."

That was Noah's father joining the conversation. Sounded to me like he had gone to the same "try to keep things calm" school of parenting as Mrs. Forman.

"Not acceptable to who?"

I had just gotten to the kitchen entryway when Noah gave his last sarcastic response. Ben, Jim, and Pete were sitting at the kitchen table, making a career out of eating scrambled eggs. Mr. Forman was also sitting at the table, holding a cup of coffee in one hand and the newspaper in the other while looking undeniably tense. Mrs. Forman stood by the stove with a flowery apron around her waist, a spatula in her hand, and her face flushed. And Noah stood in front of the refrigerator, his arms crossed over his chest, a soda in his hand, and a scowl on his face.

"Not acceptable to me."

The words left my mouth without first checking with my brain. That fight was none of my business, so I shouldn't have said a word. But I had to step in. Someone had to stop Noah from self-destructing. His family wasn't getting the job done with all their coddling because it wasn't what he needed. Besides, he was *mine* and he needed me to handle things. Instinctively, I knew that, even though I had no idea why.

Every head in the room snapped in my direction.

Jim and Pete looked terrified, Ben's mouth dropped open in shock, and Mr. and Mrs. Forman just seemed confused. But my eyes didn't focus on them. I looked at Noah. He met my gaze and his body language changed completely. He dropped his arms to his sides, relaxed his shoulders, wiped the anger from his face, and walked over to me.

"Sorry."

He was standing right next to me, his voice low enough that I wasn't sure whether anyone else could hear him. I answered at the same volume.

"I'm not the one you were yelling at, Noah. You don't owe *me* the apology."

He looked up into my eyes.

"No, I don't owe *them* an apology. You? Well, I'll give you anything you want. Always."

With that cryptic statement, he walked past me, out of the kitchen, and down the hall to his room.

WE HAD a few more post-game sleepovers before baseball season ended. It'd become assumed that I'd bunk with Noah, both because no one else wanted to sleep in his room and because Noah wouldn't let anyone else in there. It was fine with me. We had fun together. We'd stay up late, playing cards and talking about all sorts of things—books, movies, school.

I enjoyed spending time with that Noah, the one who

came out when we were alone. He was nothing like the angry, petulant kid who terrorized his family. One night when we were up late chatting, Noah told me about kickboxing and how much he enjoyed it.

The gym where he studied was downtown, which was a good hour's drive from EC North, the suburb where we lived. His parents were against him taking kickboxing, so even though they'd driven Ben and Noah all over town for soccer and baseball over the years, they'd refused to take him to the kickboxing gym. I guess maybe they thought they'd shake him from it and then he'd go back to regular team sports. Their strategy didn't work.

Noah just took the city bus, which was a bigger deal than you might realize. Emile City wasn't a public transportation town back then, and kickboxing class started at six o'clock and lasted two hours. That meant Noah stood at the bus stop downtown at night by himself. Sounds strange, right? A punk kid with an attitude who somehow had the discipline required for kickboxing and the dedication required for getting himself there and home every day. Well, that was Noah. An enigma, wrapped in a mystery, and coated in a personality-dichotomy. It'd take a lifetime to peel back all of his complicated layers, but there was nothing I'd rather have spent my time doing.

Anyway, when I'd found out about Noah's kickboxing travel schedule, I'd insisted on driving him home. I couldn't take him to his class when he first told me about it, because

I had baseball practice during that time. But after practice, I'd go home, make sure my mom was okay, and then drive downtown to pick Noah up. When baseball season ended, I added driving him to his class to my routine. I spent the couple of hours while he was training doing my homework in my car, and then I drove him home.

Noah hadn't complained about taking the bus, and he had no fear that something bad could happen to him, being out at night alone. But I was scared enough for the both of us, so when I'd insisted on driving him, he'd agreed and told me that he wouldn't turn down a chance to spend time alone with me every day, talking. Funny how happy those words made me.

CHAPTER FOUR

Noah—Present

AS SOON as I asked how long I'd been in that hospital, Clark looked over to the doctor in concern. They were both silent for a few heartbeats, and then Dr. Garcia cleared his throat.

"You've been here twenty-eight days, Noah. But..."

He hesitated, looked at Clark, and then seemed to compose himself enough to continue.

"It's not December 26, 2007, son."

Clark gasped and his face paled. His head snapped to look at Dr. Garcia.

"He, ehm, he thinks it's December 26, 2007?"

Dr. Garcia nodded. Clark turned back to me, tears filling his eyes.

"Oh, Noah."

He was trembling and his shoulders were shaking. He leaned down to me, gingerly wrapped his arms around me, and kissed my neck.

"I love you, Noah, always. I'm so sorry, sweetheart."

My eyesight was getting fuzzy again and my head hurt.

"I love you too, angel. Shhh. I'm fine. Please don't cry and don't be sorry. Just tell me the date, Clark. I can handle it."

His hand was still clutching mine, so I squeezed it, pressed my nose into the top of his head, and breathed in. I really could handle it. So long as I had Clark, I could handle anything. Losing some time didn't matter. He was safe. We were together. The rest was just unimportant detail.

Clark lifted his head and looked into my eyes. Then he turned to Dr. Garcia, who gave him a short nod. Clark breathed in deeply, cleared his throat, and met my gaze.

"It's December 14, 2010."

"I've been in this hospital for *three years*?"

Dr. Garcia responded immediately.

"No, son. Please calm down. You were in a car accident four weeks ago. That's how long you've been in the hospital. I don't know why you can't remember the past three years, but we're going to figure out the reason for your memory loss. Relax, Noah."

I closed my eyes. Okay, so I'd spent four weeks unconscious in a hospital and I couldn't remember almost three years of my life. Well, that explained why Ben and Clark looked older. My last memory of them was three years ago, so from my perspective, they *were* older. I was older.

"Sweetheart? It's going to be okay, Noah."

I nodded and opened my eyes.

"I know, angel. I'm fine, just tired and a little surprised. But you're here, so I know it's all going to be okay. Just want to rest a little now."

Clark placed his hand on my arm and kissed my cheek.

"Okay, sweetheart. I won't go anywhere. I'll be here when you wake up."

I chuckled, the idea of anything else so ridiculous I wasn't sure why he even bothered saying it.

"Of course you will, angel. Apparently I've forgotten a lot of things, but I know you'll never leave me."

A pained look crossed Clark's face. I wanted to ask about it and wipe it away, but I was so tired. Just a little nap, that was what I needed right then. A nap with my lover's warmth by my side and his spicy, earthy, vanilla scent filling me.

Clark—Past

"I DON'T know what the deal is with him. I honestly don't. He wasn't like this when he was younger. He was happy and normal."

Ben and I were sitting on the steps outside our school, eating our lunches. Ben and his parents noticed that Noah and I got along, which was the reason why Ben felt comfortable confiding in me about his brother. I think he knew I wouldn't bad-talk Noah.

"When did things change, Ben? When did he become so...so angry?"

Ben took a swig of his soda and a bite of his apple. He had a thoughtful expression on his handsome face.

"I don't know. A year or two ago, I guess. I didn't really notice it until he refused to keep playing soccer and baseball."

Noah definitely had an athletic build and Ben and his dad were both totally into sports, so it made sense that Noah used to play too.

"Why did he stop playing? I'm guessing he was probably pretty good if he's anything like his big brother."

I nudged Ben with my elbow and smiled. He gave me a light shoulder bump and a grateful look. I knew he was worried about his brother and probably appreciated being able to talk about him.

"He was way better than me, Clark. I'm not being modest, it's the truth."

"Dude, when have I ever accused you of modesty?"

"Ha-ha, asshole."

"So what happened?"

"I don't know. When he was twelve, he just refused to keep playing. Told my dad he didn't want to play traditional sports. He's been into kickboxing ever since."

That much I knew. But I'd never realized that the kickboxing had replaced other sports. I made a mental note to ask Noah about that.

"I thought things were getting better with him, Ben."

And by "thought," I meant I "knew." Because Noah had told me. I still wasn't sure how to help him or what the root cause was of his rage, but I'd tried to listen, to be there for him, and he'd said things were better at home.

"Yeah, they've been better for months now. But the last couple of days at my house have been a complete fucking nightmare. I've been locking myself in my room and blaring the stereo just so I don't have to hear them fighting."

The kickboxing gym had been closed for a couple of weeks so the owner could take a vacation. It'd worked out well for me, because it was the last week of school and not having to drive Noah back and forth downtown meant I'd had more time to study for finals. Plus, my mother was getting worse, so I'd wanted to be home with her. Of course that meant I didn't have a clue as to what had set Noah off on this latest rampage because I hadn't seen him in two weeks, which had been much harder than I would have imagined.

"Well, maybe things will calm down."

Ben shrugged.

"I hope so. It's the last day of school, which means I have to spend the next two months at home with him and my mother. At least my dad can escape to the office. Where am I supposed to hide?"

I rolled my eyes and laughed.

"Find a job or something, you lazy piece of shit. That'll get you out of the house."

He scrunched his nose in distaste.

"Why would I do that? That's *work*. Maybe I'll find a girlfriend instead. Sue Belden seems to be interested in me, and on a scale of one to ten, she's at least a seven. If I ask her out, then I can spend my summer having sex. That's preferable to working."

"Your ambition is truly inspiring, Ben."

"Bite me, dick-breath."

"Dream on, asshole."

I stood up, brushed the dirt off my shorts, crumpled my lunch bag, and threw it into the trashcan.

"That right there was nothing but net, jackass. Don't you wish you were me?"

Ben crumpled his bag, took his shot, and missed. I laughed at him.

"Oh, now that's just pathetic. Really sad. Maybe you should spend your summer with a basketball instead of focusing on your own balls. It looks like you need the practice."

Ben pushed me toward the school.

"Fuck off. That was a lunch bag, not a basketball. Besides, that's not my best sport and you know it."

"No? What, they've made masturbation a sport now? Is it Olympic level or just college?"

He gave me a fake laugh and pretended to wipe tears from his eyes. Then he put his arm around my shoulder and leaned on me as we walked back into school to finish our last three classes before summer break.

"You're too funny, Lehman. You know that? Have you

considered a life of stand-up comedy?"

IT WAS summer vacation and I was glad to have a break from classwork and sports. I'd considered getting a summer job, but it looked like my mom only had a few months left and I wanted to spend whatever time I could with her. Sometimes we watched movies, sometimes I read books and magazines to her, but most of the time we just talked, trying to squeeze in all the memories we could in the little time we had left together. I'd miss her like crazy when she passed, but I tried to focus on how lucky I was to have such a wonderful mother.

My mom went to sleep really early every night and we had hospice set up, so I was able to leave to hang out with friends without worrying that she wouldn't get what she needed. On the Saturday after classes ended, Ben and I had plans to go to a party at a friend's house. I got to his place at eight o'clock to pick him up. As soon as he answered the door, I knew something was wrong.

"Oh shit, Clark. I'm sorry that I forgot to call you. Turns out I can't go out tonight. Things are a fucking mess around here."

"Benjamin Isaac Forman, watch your language!"

That was his mother's voice coming from around the corner. Ben rolled his eyes and whispered to me.

"Seriously? You know some of the crap my brother

pulls and I'm getting a lecture for saying shit and fuck. Whatever."

He raked his fingers through his already messy hair. His clothes looked crumpled and slept-in and he had dark circles under his bloodshot eyes. I'd never seen Ben look so disheveled. I didn't even realize that was possible for Mister Always-just-so.

"What's going on, Ben? You look like hell."

He waved me in and closed the door behind us.

"Charming as always, Lehman. How do you do it? Is that type of flattery the reason why you can't seem to get laid?"

Well, at least he was making jokes. That was a good sign.

"I'm not trying to get into your pants, Ben. Is that type of cluelessness the reason why you can't seem to stop getting slapped?"

Ben grabbed his dick through his pants and squeezed it.

"Suck mine."

I patted his back.

"You're really reaching into your fantasy material now, friend, best you get over it quickly, because my mouth on your dick is never going to happen."

He must have been truly tired because he let my wise-ass remark go without a retort.

"You want a soda or something?"

I followed him into the kitchen, where his father was slumped in a chair, talking on the phone and twisting the cord between his fingers anxiously.

"Thirty-six hours. Because I don't want him to have a record with the police, that's why. I don't think anybody took him. He's just mad at us, so he's trying to punish us by scaring the shit out of us."

Mr. Forman quickly looked at Ben and me standing by the fridge and mouthed a silent *"don't tell your mother I said shit."* Then he went back to his conversation.

"Yeah, thanks, Harvey. If you hear anything, give us a call. I know. If he doesn't come home soon, that's what we'll do."

He hung up the phone, looking defeated.

"Nothing?"

Ben said it less like a question and more like a resigned comment. His dad raised himself from the chair, walked by us, patted Ben's shoulder, shook his head no, and left the room. I tried not to panic and waited quietly for Ben to fill me in, wondering if he could hear my racing heart or if it was only loud in my own body.

"We don't know where Noah is."

"I heard your dad say thirty-six hours on the phone. That's how long he's been gone?"

Ben nodded.

"Yeah."

I chewed on my nail and willed my heart to slow down.

"Has he ever been gone this long before?"

Ben sat down, folded his arms on the table, and dropped his head down onto them.

"Nah. He usually just sneaks out at night. He's never been gone even a whole day. I'm freaking out, man. My parents don't want to call the cops because they don't want everyone to know about our family issues. But between all the fighting the last few days and now the disappearing act, I'm really worried about him."

I was worried too. And not just because it wasn't right for a thirteen-year-old kid to be gone that long. I cared about Noah. He mattered to me. My stomach hurt with a feeling I recognized as fear. My chest ached too, with a feeling I couldn't identify. I stood up and nudged Ben.

"Get changed. We're going to find your brother."

He looked up at me.

"How?"

"By going door-to-door to his friends' houses. One of them is bound to spill just to get us out of there."

Ben immediately got to his feet, looking hopeful for the first time since I'd gotten there.

"Yeah. That's a good idea. I know some of the people he hangs out with from our school. I always thought it was weird that he's friends with people who are so much older than him, but at least they're not high school dropouts like his other friends."

Ben was right. Noah's circle of friends was odd to say

the least. Ben and I hung out with other jocks. We partied—meaning drinking beer with our buddies and guys making out with their girlfriends. Noah hung out with people who didn't fit a traditional social group and, if the rumors had any semblance of truth in them, those people partied by doing drugs and having indiscriminate sex.

Some of Noah's friends were in high school, some had finished high school, some had dropped out, and all of them were wild in some way—weird hair, tattoos, piercings, criminal records, STDs, abortions, fights, drug use. I found it strange that those people let a middle-school kid hang out with them, but Noah was charismatic, unique, and nothing like other kids his age. Heck, I enjoyed hanging out with him too. In fact, there was nobody else I'd rather be with.

I couldn't lose Noah. He had to be all right. *Had* to be. I just needed to find him.

CHAPTER FIVE

Noah—Present

I HEARD their quiet whispers as I started waking.

"Because I was in the room when Noah told Dr. Garcia about it, and he was very clear that his brother and the rest of his family aren't welcome here."

"Are you sure, Nurse? He might appreciate knowing that Ben and his parents keep calling and coming by."

"I'm just telling you what happened, sir. His brother was here, they had a fight, and Noah passed out again for hours. It was panic city around here. Then he woke up and kicked his brother out of the room."

I started feeling guilty about listening in on the conversation without their knowledge, so I opened my eyes and joined in.

"I'd say that you shouldn't talk about a man behind his back, but I'm right here in the room, so I'm not sure this counts."

Clark rushed over to me, brushed my hair out of my face, and stroked my cheek. His brow was furrowed in concern as he looked me over carefully.

"Did we wake you, Noah? I'm sorry. I know you need your sleep."

I shook my head and reveled in his touch. It wasn't just because I was in the hospital. Clark had always been super loving and affectionate with me. Well, since he finally agreed to date me, anyway. Dated, that was a laugh—we hadn't ever dated. We'd gone from friendship to a lifetime commitment in one glorious moment. The memory of that day made my dick stir, which hurt.

"No. I've been sleeping so much that it's nice to be conscious now and then. Listen, Clark, I don't have the energy to deal with my brother and my parents right now. Can we please just skip the whole 'they're your family, they love you' talk? At least for a little while?"

I must have looked really bad, because Clark actually agreed with me and stopped trying to talk me into mending fences with my shithead brother and the rest of my family. Well, I suppose that was the silver lining to being stuck in a hospital bed.

Now, for the bad part—there was a wet feeling against my thigh.

"Umm. Something doesn't feel right, doesn't feel good."

I shifted as best as I could.

"Where, Noah? Where does it hurt?"

The nurse came over and nudged Clark out of the way.

She started looking at my head and my eyes, before I could get her attention.

"No, not up here. My leg is…wet or something."

She lifted the sheet, then quickly put it down.

"It looks like you have a leak in your catheter bag, sir. We'll need to change the bag." Then she turned to Clark. "You can wait outside, Mr. Lehman."

My heart rate immediately quickened, and not in a good way. It felt like an elephant had just sat down on my chest.

"Don't leave me, angel."

Clark took my hand in his, gave me a reassuring squeeze, and turned to the nurse.

"I'll stay right here. I need you to explain why you're changing the bag. He's awake now. It seems to me that you can remove the catheter all together."

The nurse looked a bit startled by the firm tone in Clark's voice, but she recovered quickly and answered him.

"Well, you'll have to ask the doctor, but I imagine the catheter is still necessary because Mr. Forman can't walk yet, so he can't make it to the toilet, and he still has limited arm mobility, so negotiating the bedpan is probably too challenging at this point."

Clark furrowed his brow, looked down at me appraisingly, then back to the nurse.

"I'd like to talk to the doctor. I can help him use the bedpan until he's able to get to the toilet, and then I'll help with that. There's no reason for him to have a catheter any longer. And I want the IV out too. I'll make sure he gets enough fluids and takes whatever medications he needs."

I know some people might be embarrassed or uncomfortable with the idea of their partner doing those things, but I was just grateful. It felt so good to have him take care of me. And we'd always done that for each other—colds, flus, hangovers. We took turns rubbing backs, making soup, cleaning vomit. Hospitals and catheters were new to me, but not to Clark, who'd helped his mother with much worse. Besides, it wouldn't be the first time Clark had held my dick to help me take a leak, just the first time he had to do it because of broken legs instead of too much booze.

Oh no, thinking of Clark's hand on my dick for any reason whatsoever was an inevitable turn-on. Hard dicks and catheters don't mix. I fidgeted, tried to will down my erection, and wondered when I could get out of that hospital and into bed with Clark. Ugh, bed and Clark in the same thought. Damn erection was never going down.

Clark—Past

"DUDE, YOU drive like my ass chews gum."

I was driving and Ben was navigating, using the school

directory to find addresses for Noah's friends who went to our high school. Every house we'd gone to up to that point was a dead end. Either (a) his friend was out for the night and the friend's parents had no idea where or (b) the friend was home and told us to get lost.

"Bite me, asswipe," I growled, then punched Ben's arm.

"Is that an offer, baby-cakes?" He held his hand over his heart and batted his eyelashes in an exaggerated way.

"You wish, *baby-cakes*. Whose place is this again?" I rolled my eyes at him.

"Sally Jones."

I pulled up to the curb and put the car in park.

"Yeah, I know her. She was in my history class. Seemed nice."

Ben dug some gum out of his pocket and offered me a piece. I shook my head.

"Yeah, real *nice*."

There was an odd inflection in his voice.

"What do you mean?"

He looked at me to see whether I was kidding.

"Dude, she's fucked half the senior class. Total slut. On a scale of one to ten, she's no higher than a four point five, so you might have a shot. Maybe if you pork her, she'll tell you where my brother is. I'm going to take a nap while you get the job done. What do you need, like thirty, sixty seconds, max?"

I punched his stomach. He hunched over in pain.

"Umph!"

"Quit thinking about my sexual prowess, man. How many times do I have to tell you that you're not my type? And I'm going to do you a favor and pretend you didn't just say pork."

"Whatever, Clark. Premature ejaculation isn't considered prowess. And everybody loves pork. Haven't you heard that it's the new white meat?" He squeezed his dick and waggled his eyebrows.

"Oh, you did *not* just say that. I might never be able to eat pork again."

Ben laughed.

"You can eat my pork any time, Clarky. Now get the fuck out there and talk to slutty Sally."

I got out of the car, walked up the sidewalk, and was about to knock when the door opened.

"Hey, Sally, I'm—"

"You're looking for Noah. I know. I've been warned."

I raised my eyebrows in question.

"Tim Berger called me after you went to his place. And Rachel MacCallister. And Jordy Stein. Should I keep going?"

I rubbed the sidewalk with my toe. It was hopeless. Noah's friends were closing ranks and we weren't getting anywhere.

"No need to keep listing them off. I know where I've been tonight. What I want to know is where Noah's been. Or, more specifically, where he is."

I looked down and tried to meet her eyes.

"I'm worried about him, Sally. He's my friend."

She seemed to be considering my words and then she nodded.

"I know. He's told me that. I haven't been partying for a while because of...well, you know..."

I didn't know, but it didn't seem like interrupting her at that point was going to get me any closer to Noah.

"Anyway, I haven't seen him, but from what I've heard, he's on a major bender. More than usual. I, umm, I'm worried too. I'll tell you where they're partying tonight, but you *cannot* say you heard it from me, got it?"

I nodded furiously. Something that had been constricting my heart released with the knowledge that I was going to find Noah, make sure he was okay, wrap my arms around him and feel him breathing against me. Whoa. Where did that last thought come from?

"Yeah, sure, whatever. I just want to find him, Sally. I won't tell anyone how I knew where to look."

She gave me the address for an apartment outside of town where one of their friends lived and I hustled back to the car. Ben had actually managed to fall asleep. All the anxiety over his brother must have totally drained him. As soon as I closed the door, his head snapped up and he looked at me expectantly.

"I got an address. Apparently there's a party at some guy named Pat's place. He doesn't go to our school."

Ben sat up straight.

"Excellent work. So did you have to eat her out for that or was a straight fuck enough?"

Another hard punch in the stomach from me and a satisfying groan from Ben later and we were off to get my Noah.

"NOT A chance, douche bag."

Ben had spent the past five minutes trying to talk his way into the apartment where Sally had sent us, but the guy inside refused to open the door. The lack of sleep combined with Ben's naturally aggressive personality and the stress he'd been under since Noah had disappeared were creating a potentially problematic situation. Ben had gone from knocking quietly and asking nicely to banging on the door and demanding entrance with words definitely not rated E for Everyone.

"I'm fucking going to break the motherfucking door down if you don't fucking open it right fucking now, motherfucker!"

I had been standing back, letting Ben take the lead, but I came to the realization his approach wasn't working. I moved forward and caught his hand in the air before he could continue the door pounding, and pulled him away from the apartment.

"Okay, first of all, you need to learn some new adjectives. Secondly, you need to calm down, Ben, or someone will call the police, and then your parents will have two kids to worry about."

He yanked his hand out of my grip and glared at the door.

"Those cocksuckers aren't going to call the police, Clark. I'm sure they have drugs and who knows what else in there."

I tried to meet his eyes and keep my voice calm, hoping it would have the same effect on him.

"I'm not talking about them, Ben. I'm talking about their neighbors. Surely there are some people living in this apartment complex who don't have contraband in their places and they probably don't appreciate the noise we're making. Not to mention the fact that you're not getting anywhere by yelling through the door."

He rubbed his face with the palms of his hands and I got a better look at the damage he'd done to his hands trying to get Noah's friend to let us in. His knuckles were raw and bloody. Once the adrenaline wore off, he was going to be hurting.

"Well, what do you suggest, Clark? I'm not leaving him here."

The thought of leaving Noah in that apartment hadn't even crossed my mind. Just hearing Ben say it exacerbated the knot in my stomach that had relaxed when I'd gotten the address from Sally. I chewed my bottom lip and tried to figure out what to do. I didn't have any brilliant plans.

"I don't know, Ben. Just calm down a little, okay? I'll try talking to Pat, or whatever his name is, while you get it together."

Ben didn't reject the idea, so I quickly walked back to the apartment, took a deep breath, and knocked quietly.

"What part of fuck off aren't you getting, asshole? Have you been hit in the head too many times with a ball or something? I'm not letting you in, so get lost."

I got close to the door so I could keep my voice fairly low but still make sure it traveled inside.

"Look, we're not trying to cause a problem for you. We're just worried about Noah Forman. Please let us in so we can talk to him. Please."

There was a long silence and then I heard the guy's voice come through the door. He was no longer yelling.

"You're Clark, right?"

I had no idea how the guy knew my name, but I couldn't be bothered to care. I only wanted to get to Noah. I needed to know that he was okay. I was honestly starting to feel sick, and if I didn't get to him soon, I thought I'd probably throw up.

"Yeah, that's right."

"You can come in, but the other guy stays outside."

I looked over at Ben. His face was red with anger, his knuckles were bleeding, and he looked like he was on the verge of a full-on breakdown. I turned back to the door and spoke through it to the guy who'd said he'd let me in alone.

"Okay, I'll come in without Ben. Thanks. I appreciate it."

I walked over to my friend, put my hands on his shoulders, and gathered my nerve.

"Ben, he's going to let me in there, but you can't come with me."

His entire body tensed.

"Why the fuck not? He's my fucking brother! And I don't want you in that fucking apartment."

Seriously, when this whole thing was over, I'd have to teach Ben a few new expletives.

"I know, Ben. Look, he's probably just trying to save face because he's been fighting with you. What does it matter which one of us goes into the apartment? The important thing is that we get Noah out of there and take him home. Right?"

Ben nodded reluctantly and grumbled something under his breath. That was the best reaction I could hope for considering the situation, so I took it and went back to the apartment. Another quiet knock and the door opened a crack. I smiled weakly at the eye peering at me from behind the door.

"Just me. Thanks again for letting me in."

He stepped back and I squeezed in through the doorway. The guy who'd opened the door was huge, tattooed, pierced, and—based on the smell coming off him—drunk as all get out. The apartment was small, dark, and putrid. There was something in the air that burned my eyes and lungs. My natural reaction to all of those things should have been to turn tail and get the hell out of that nasty, scary place. But that wasn't what I wanted to do. No, the only thing I wanted in that moment was Noah.

CHAPTER SIX

Noah—Present

THE NURSE brought over the attending physician, and after a long conversation in which Clark insisted they remove the various tubes connected to my body, my dick burned, but it was free of the damned catheter, and my arm was no longer attached to anything. Clark tucked me into the bed after the hospital staff changed the sheets. He brushed my hair back and kissed my forehead.

"You tell me when you need to go and I'll bring the bedpan over, sweetheart. Did you hear the doctor say it'll be uncomfortable for the next few times?"

I nodded and cupped the back of his head with my left hand.

"Didn't think we'd be having this type of conversation until fifty years from now. Sorry about this, angel. It's not a fun way to spend the holidays."

Clark kissed my forehead again, combed his fingers gently through my hair, and whispered in my ear, "Shhhh. I'm with you, Noah. There's no better way to spend the holidays or any other day. And I don't mind doing this. You know how much I love taking care of you. Speaking of taking care of you, it looks to me like you need a shave and a manicure."

I slowly raised my left hand to my face and grazed my fingers over my jaw. Wow. That was the longest my beard had ever gotten. And my nails did look unruly.

"That sounds good, Clark. Thank you."

He went to the nurses' station to ask for equipment and then came back into the room.

"They're getting us an electric razor to shave off the bulk and I'll do the rest with a regular razor. I have the nail clippers now, so I can start on your hands and feet."

And that was what he did. He held my hands gently, one at a time. Massaged my palms and clipped each nail until they were all squared off. My dick was still sore from the catheter removal, but that didn't stop me from getting hard. The man I loved was with me, touching me, and there was just no way my body wasn't going to react to him. After all, I'd been reacting to him pretty much from the time I figured out what my dick was for.

"Thanks, angel. That felt really good."

He looked down at the tent in the sheet and his blue eyes darkened and smoldered. He leaned down to kiss me. The kiss was soft at first, gentle, but then it got more passionate, our tongues met and danced, and we both moaned. When we finally separated, I whimpered at the loss and Clark was panting.

"Okay, sweetheart, the pedicure's next."

He adjusted his hard-on, walked to the bottom of the bed, folded the sheet up so one of my feet was exposed, then rubbed the sole, ball, arch, and heel.

"Mmm. Feels so good, Clark."

After the massage, he clipped the nails on that foot, then covered it, and moved to my other foot for a repeat performance.

"You're so wonderful to me."

He leaned down for another kiss, but we got interrupted by the nurse bringing the shaving supplies. Clark took his time, shaving off the heaviest part of the hair on my face in waves, until just stubble remained. Then he wet a washcloth with hot water and laid it over my cheeks to soften the remaining hair. After that, he covered my face with shaving cream, and slowly shaved it off. A final wipe-down with a clean washcloth and he was done.

"There you go, Noah. All smooth. It's nice to see your beautiful face again. Although I must say that the bearded look was sexy and gorgeous too."

He meant those words. I knew he did. But Clark was actually the beautiful one. My features were much harsher than his. I felt so lucky. How many people had a partner who loved them enough to take care of them like that and thought they were beautiful even when they were laid up in a hospital bed?

"Thank you, angel. Can I have another kiss?"

Teary eyes met mine and my lover leaned down and kissed my lips. Gentle, soft, loving. Damn, he felt good.

"All this activity wore me out, Clark. Okay if I take a little nap?"

He moved his chair back over to its spot by the head of my bed. Guess the hospital staff moved it when they were changing the sheets. Then he sat next to me, took my hands in his, and kissed me tenderly.

"Sleep, sweetheart. I'll be right here by your side when you wake up. Forever."

Yes, he would.

Clark—Past

ONCE MY eyes adjusted to the darkness, I looked around the filthy apartment and saw people in various states of dress— or undress, depending on your viewpoint—making out on the couches. I recognized some of them from school, but others were unfamiliar. There were people lying on the floor, sleeping or passed out. A couple of guys were sitting in front of the TV with glazed looks on their faces. And two girls were sucking face in the corner. I hated the thought that Noah had been in that place for almost two days.

I restrained my body's need to retch and turned to the

guy who let me in.

"Where, um, where's Noah?"

He moved his chin toward a door at one end of the room.

"Thanks."

I walked to that door, pushed past it, and then I saw him. He was sitting at a table, flicking a lighter with one hand and heating a piece of aluminum foil he was holding with his other hand. Smoke or vapor was rising from the foil and he was holding what looked like a piece of plastic in his mouth in the midst of it.

"Noah?"

His red eyes rose up to me and I almost lost it and burst into tears. He looked tired, dirty, and agitated, but that wasn't what killed me. What hurt was the sadness that poured off him. I walked over to him, squatted down by his feet, and covered both his hands with mine, effectively stopping the flame on the lighter. Then I lowered the foil to the table, pulled Noah off his chair and onto my lap, and rocked him in my arms.

"What are you doing, Noah?"

My voice was barely a whisper, but his head was tucked under my chin, so he heard me.

"Chasing the white dragon."

Call me naïve, but I hadn't ever heard that phrase and I didn't know what it meant. Not that the specifics mattered. I had the general idea—he ran away from home and had been holed up in that apartment, doing drugs. What I wanted to know was why—why had he been fighting with his parents that past week, why had he run away from home, and why was he doing drugs?

I kicked myself for not having asked him what the deal was with his anger before it'd gotten to that point. I'd been spending hours with him every week for months. I thought he knew that I was there for him, that I cared, that he could talk to me. I rubbed circles on his back, held him tightly against my chest, and continued the rocking motion.

"What happened, Noah? Talk to me."

He folded himself closer to my body.

"I can't take it anymore. I can't. I thought I could stick it out, you know? So they wouldn't hate me. Just until I turn eighteen and then I can tell them to fuck off. But that's, like, four more years. I can't keep this up for that long because keeping them from hating me only makes me hate myself. And how can I escape myself, huh? How can I do that?"

I tried to concentrate on what he was telling me, tried to put it together with what I knew about Noah and his family. But I was having trouble following what he was saying. I was pretty sure the "they" he was referring to were his parents. And I gathered the drugs were his way of trying to escape himself. After that, I was totally lost.

"Why would they hate you? Your parents love you, Noah. I'm sorry if you can't see that, but you have to believe me. I've seen how they are with you."

He scoffed.

"That's because they don't know me. It's pretty fucking ironic, isn't it? I can do anything on earth to push them away—drugs, sneaking out, cussing at them—and they'll just talk to me or ground me, all the while they'll say they love me. But if they knew the truth, I'd be out on my ass."

Nothing. I had nothing in the way of understanding what his "truth" was. But he was right about the rest of it. Noah was the most ill-behaved kid I knew. He flat-out terrorized his family. I couldn't even begin to imagine what my mother would do if I pulled half the shit that Noah got away with scot-free.

"Well, I'm here because I care about you, Noah. The real you. Please tell me what happened. Ben said you'd been fighting with your parents all week and then you just left. What did they do?"

He sighed and clutched my waist.

"They didn't do anything they haven't done a million times before. I'm just sick of being such a chickenshit. My mom came home from the grocery store on Monday and she was all agitated. I guess she had run into a friend who works with Sally Jones's mom. Anyway, she told my mom about how Sally got knocked up and doesn't know who the father is and about how her parents are forcing all our friends to take paternity tests. So then my mom asked me if I'm the father."

Oh dear God. A father at thirteen. That was a nightmare. Noah's parents could help financially, but I didn't think they'd be willing to help raise the baby. Plus they were always concerned about how their friends perceived them, and if word got out that their teenage son was going to be a father, they'd be furious.

"Oh, Noah. I'm so sorry."

"It's ironic, right? My mom's freaking out, thinking I knocked up some girl. Meanwhile, I'm like one of the few guys in our group who clearly isn't a candidate. I told her that, you know? I said I wasn't on the paternity test list. But she didn't believe me. She said she knew I was having sex.

"And what was I supposed to say? 'Yeah, that's true but unless they've made some serious advancements in male anatomy, nobody I fuck can get pregnant?' That's a surefire way to get my ass thrown out of the house, so I didn't tell her. Better to have her think I'm going to be a dad than to have her know I'm queer. Fucking priceless, right?"

He's gay? The way he was talking, it was like he assumed I knew. Clearly, Ben had no idea and Noah had never told me, so I didn't know why he thought I had a clue. Maybe it was because the first time I'd met him he'd said he was giving blow jobs in that rainbow room, but, honestly, I'd just thought it was some weird party thing he did with his friends. I didn't realize he was gay.

"Why do you think they'd kick you out if they knew? There's nothing wrong with being gay. You realize that, right?"

Based on what he was saying, I assumed he hated

himself because of his sexual orientation and maybe that was the reason for his self-destructive behavior. There were groups for gay teens, and I figured I could find one and get Noah some help. I didn't want him to keep using drugs or worse.

"Of course I know that. I love being gay. It's my parents that have the problem. You know how they are."

Yeah, I did know. They were nice, educated, church-going people who put up with an endless barrage of crap from Noah. The word "long-suffering" came to mind when I thought of Mr. and Mrs. Forman. I decided we were at a place where honesty was the best policy.

"Noah, I like your parents. Think about what they put up with from you."

My legs were falling asleep in my squatting position, but Noah was shivering and holding on to me for dear life, so I didn't want to let him go. I unfolded my legs and sat on my ass. Then I pushed myself back against the wall and kept cradling Noah.

"Oh sure, they seem all nice and caring, but you should hear what they say. A few years ago, I was at the mall with my dad and two guys were holding hands. He gave them dirty looks, pulled me away like they were going to hurt me or something, and started talking real loud about faggots and how they shouldn't be allowed to act that way in front of decent people. And that wasn't out of character for him. He says stuff like that all the time.

"And my mom isn't any better. Like one time we were watching the news and they were talking about the anniversary of the Stonewall riots, you know the gay civil rights thing in New York? Anyway, my mom flipped the channel and said they should have just killed them all."

I had no idea. I'd heard Ben make derogatory comments about gay people now and then, but I'd always thought it was just locker-room talk, nothing serious. But to be a gay kid growing up in a house where your family said those types of things had to hurt.

"Oh, Noah. I didn't know."

I tightened my hold around him so I could give his body a reassuring squeeze. He sighed contentedly.

"Yeah, well you don't spend that much time with them. If you did, you'd hear their crap. Plus your mom is so cool you probably don't realize how unaccepting other parents can be. I bet your mother joined PFLAG or something when you came out."

My mother was wonderful and accepting. I'd told Noah all about her during our car rides back and forth to kickboxing. Wait—Noah thought I was gay? Why would he think that? I mean, I hadn't ever had a girlfriend, or any real interest in girls for that matter. But that was just because I was busy with school and sports. It didn't mean anything. Did it?

CHAPTER SEVEN

Noah—Present

"OH GOOD, you're awake."

Ummm. No, not really. Eyes still closed here. Not exactly the international sign for awake.

"Well, I am now."

I opened my eyes to see a new face. Cute guy, younger than me. And by that, I mean younger than I used to be back when I actually had a decent memory. It would take a while to remember that over the past four weeks I'd somehow skipped from age twenty-four to age twenty-seven, with no memory of the years in between.

"I, uh, I get off shift soon and I wanted to make sure you got your sponge bath."

He was leering at me and there was a distinct bulge in his scrub pants. If it weren't for that horrible antiseptic hospital smell, I would have sworn I'd just stumbled onto a porn shoot.

Just then, the bathroom door opened, and Clark stepped out, drying his hands on a paper towel. He looked at me and then at the… What do you call the people who give sponge baths in hospitals? Was he a nurse? An aide?

"Did you wake him up?"

Clark was scowling. Since the second he'd stepped into that hospital, Clark had been like a pit bull, I swear. Making sure I got enough sleep. Bringing me food from outside the hospital because he insisted it was more nutritious. Reading every lab result and scan, and then spending hours on his laptop researching what they all meant. At least I assumed it was hours, I was still sleeping most of the day, so it wasn't like I was conscious for it. Awake or asleep, though, I appreciated him, appreciated the way he always took care of me, looked out for me. I was grateful for Clark every day of my life.

"No, angel. I was already awake."

I figured the aide deserved a break. He probably worked hard and there was no reason for him to suffer the wrath of my lover for committing the heinous crime of sleep interruptus.

"Oh. Okay then."

Clark threw the paper towel into the trashcan, walked over to my bed, and took his usual seat by my side. He stroked his hand over my forehead and brushed my hair out of my face. The adoring look in his eyes when he gazed at me took my breath away and melted my heart. Aide guy cleared his throat.

"It's time for me to give Mr. Forman his bath, so you can wait outside."

No way would Clark let that happen. He was only one step less possessive of me than I was of him. Okay, maybe more than just one step. What can I say? He's mine. *Mine*. And I don't take kindly to anyone making a mistake about that.

"You know what, why don't you just leave the cart with the water and washcloths here? My partner can handle the bath. We won't need any other help."

"Bath?"

Clark looked surprised. Aide guy couldn't leave well enough alone. He walked closer to the bed, put his hand on my arm, leered at me again, and licked his lips.

"I don't mind, Mr. Forman. It's my job."

I bit the inside of my cheek to keep from laughing. Was this guy coming on to me? I was in a hospital bed, for Christ's sake. And my partner was sitting right next to me. That was just tacky. Oh, and unprofessional.

"Well, I mind. I don't want anyone other than my lover near my personal bits, 'kay?"

Aide guy grumbled something under his breath, but he cleared out of the room.

"What do you think, angel? You up for giving me a full-body rubdown?"

I looked up at Clark and noticed his flushed face, his heavy breathing, and his erection threatening to poke a hole in his jeans. I cupped his cock and gave it a squeeze.

"That answers that question, doesn't it? You're really up for it. Maybe we can find a way to make this whole bath experience mutually satisfying."

Clark moaned.

"Getting to touch you is more satisfying than anything else I've ever experienced, Noah. You sure you don't mind?"

"Umm, mind having the man I love rub his wet, soapy hands all over my body? It'll be a sacrifice, but I think I'll power through."

I was trying to be funny, but Clark vibrated with need.

"I love you, Noah."

He leaned down and kissed me. It was a soft kiss, a press of his lips against mine. But the familiar electricity jolted through me and I swiped my tongue across the crease in his lips. He opened to me and I pressed my tongue into his mouth, sweeping it around, enjoying his flavor. He sucked me in and whimpered, one hand making its way to my hair, the other to the back of my neck.

We twisted and turned, tongues wrestling, lips pressing. By the time we separated for oxygen, my sheet was tented and the front of Clark's pants was forming a wet spot.

"Damn, angel!"

Clark leaned his forehead down against mine, panting. He stroked my cheek.

"Damn is right. It's like magic with you, Noah. Always has been. Every time, from the beginning."

I rubbed my cheek against his.

"We're a sorry pair, aren't we, angel?"

He did it for me, really did it for me, always had, but

being one breath away from blowing my load from nothing but a kiss was extreme. I didn't think I'd even been that worked up the first time we'd fooled around. Well, I had been in the hospital for weeks. And before my first time with Clark, I'd no clue how good the reality would be; how much better than any fantasy I'd ever had.

"What do you mean, Noah?"

I chuckled and palmed his hard cock.

"Keep us apart for a few weeks, and we practically come in our pants at the first touch of each other. Do you think it's like this for other people too?"

It was a rhetorical question. He wouldn't know because he'd never been with another guy. I had, but not many and certainly not in anything resembling a relationship.

"Do you wonder about what it's like for other people, Noah? What it'd be like to be with other people?"

I'd had a few friends ask me that over the years—whether I thought I'd eventually feel like I missed out because Clark and I had gotten together when I was eighteen. I'd never understood that question.

"No, angel, I don't. Why would I choose to be with anyone else when I have you? You're the only guy I've ever wanted and that's never going to change. I love you, Clark."

He kissed me deeply, then bit and gnawed on my bottom lip, my throat, and my earlobe. Fuck, that was hot. He looked into my eyes, searching for something. Then he rested his head against my shoulder and sighed.

"No, sweetheart. I don't think it's always like this for people. You make my entire body come alive, Noah. I want you with everything that I am, all the time."

My heart ached with the power of my love for him.

"Me too. The way I feel about you is so...big, all-consuming. I need you, angel."

"I need you too, Noah. More than anything."

Clark tucked some towels under me, then looked through the supplies on the cart the nurse had brought in. While he was getting things organized for my sponge bath, I was sitting in the hospital bed trying not to come in my gown from the mere anticipation of him touching me.

He stepped over to the bed with a wet washcloth, and I noticed his dick was still hard. I pulled his face down to mine for a few more kisses, slow and sweet. Suddenly, I felt wetness against my cheek. I hadn't ever remembered seeing Clark cry before that time in the hospital. Not when his mother died, not when my brother deserted him, not when his friends harassed him, and not when my parents threatened him.

But during the last few days, it seemed like a regular occurrence. I'd wake up from a nap to find him watching me with tears in his eyes. Or I'd say something innocuous, like just now, and he'd cry. It didn't make sense to me, but I knew we had to get out of that hospital. It wasn't good for either of us.

Clark—Past

I SHOOK my head to clear the thoughts about why Noah thought I was gay. I would have plenty of time to think about myself once I got Noah calmed down and somewhere safe.

"Look, this drugging, rebelling shit isn't helping. I get that you think you're punishing your parents or something, but you're just hurting yourself. You're thirteen years old. I know you're smart, really smart, and way more mature than other people your age. So I'm going to ask you to step back and think about what you've been doing. Really think about it, Noah. When you do, you'll realize this has to stop. The drugs, the sneaking out, the...the, ehm, random sex. It has to stop, Noah, or you won't make it to eighteen. Do you get that?"

He sighed into my neck and nodded his head.

"Yeah, I get it, Clark."

Thank goodness.

"Tell me one thing, though. I understand the issues with the drugs, maybe even the sneaking out. But the sex? What if I always use condoms? The random sex prohibition, is that because you're saying I should have someone steady? Like one guy? A boyfriend?"

Was that what I was saying? Truly, I was focused on the fact that he was too young to be having sex at all. I mean, I was four years older than Noah and I hadn't had sex, so that meant he was too young. But would saying that help? He'd been having sex for who knew how long and I gathered there were multiple partners involved. Was there really any chance I could talk him into stopping altogether? That seemed unlikely.

Maybe saying he should get a boyfriend would be the right thing. That had to be less harmful than what he had been doing and it was a much more realistic option. So why couldn't I get the words out? Why did it hurt to think about him with anyone, even a steady guy?

"Clark?"

I realized that I hadn't answered his question.

"Oh. Sorry. Yeah?"

"What I'm trying to ask you in a not-so-subtle way is whether I have a chance with you."

Me? He wanted me to be his boyfriend? Some part of me felt warmed by that, but I had no idea why.

"Noah, you're too young for me. I'm going to be a senior next year and you're still in middle school. That's not okay. Plus, in six months I'll be eighteen, at which point things would be flat-out illegal, in addition to being immoral."

Really? That was my answer? Not, "I'm not gay" or "I'm flattered, but I'm not into guys"? And what the hell was the "in six months" comment? Like if I did date him, it'd definitely be a long-term relationship?

"Yeah, I figured you'd say something like that. Well, I'd try to talk you into it, remind you about how you said I'm mature for my age, tell you I've been with guys older than you, but I know it's hopeless. You've got a ton of self-control and you're much too upstanding to fool around with a younger guy. I can't even be pissed, because those are some of the things I admire about you."

The door to the kitchen opened and the guy who had let me into the apartment came in.

"Noah, man, you've got to get your brother to back the fuck down. He's yelling outside again. If he doesn't stop, then one of the neighbors is bound to complain. The landlord already hates me, and if another panda car gets sent over here, I'll get evicted."

Noah sighed and slowly untangled himself from me.

"Yeah, sorry, P. I'll just take off. Thanks for letting me crash here."

"It's cool. See you later, man."

Noah's friend left and the two of us got up and stretched our legs.

"So how bad is it at my house?"

I thought about how Noah's parents had behaved when I had been at his house earlier that night.

"Not that bad, really."

He laughed as we walked out of the kitchen.

"Figures. I'm gone for two days without a word, I'll come home smelling like smoke and alcohol, and they'll probably just tell me not to do it again. But if they knew I like cock, they'd send me to a fucking retraining camp."

He rubbed his palms over his face.

"I don't know how much longer I can handle this,

Clark."

I put my arm around him and led him out of that disgusting apartment.

"I don't have the answers yet, but remember that you're not alone. I'm going to help you, Noah. We'll figure this out together."

CHAPTER EIGHT

Noah—Present

"OKAY, SWEETHEART. I have the bed covered with towels. Now we need to take off your gown."

I looked up at Clark's flushed face. He was getting me ready for my sponge bath. After he took the sheet and blanket off me, he ran his gaze up and down my body, spending extra time on the area where my gown was significantly higher than the rest because of the tent being formed by my hard dick.

"Go ahead and take it off, angel. But I have to warn you, the amount of cleaning required might increase. I want you so bad, Clark. I think I'm going to explode."

His eyes darkened and he adjusted his cock in his pants.

"Do you really want *me*, Noah?"

He had walked up to the head of the bed and was leaning over, his face inches from mine. I was panting at that point. The spicy, earthy, vanilla smell of his skin alone was going to set me off, I swear. When we'd first gotten together,

I was sure that scent came from a bottle, because no human could smell that damn good naturally. But after living together all those years, I knew that it really was pure Clark. Delicious.

"Damn, angel. Can't you tell how much I want you?"

I was gasping for air and my entire body was tense, trying to hold off the inevitable.

"I want to see."

He reached behind me and untied the gown. His warm fingers brushed against my skin and I moaned. Then he pulled one sleeve gingerly down my arm and did the same with the other arm, his fingers caressing my skin as he went.

"Clark!"

He froze.

"Am I hurting you, Noah?"

"God, no. Feels so good, angel. So damn good to have you touching me."

The look on his face was hard to identify—relief or surprise, maybe. I wasn't sure. I was having trouble concentrating because he was inching the gown down my chest, then gently lifting it off my body. I focused on breathing and not coming, but when his fingers barely grazed my cock as he moved the gown, I lost it.

"Oh! Clark, Clark!"

I cried out in surprise and satisfaction as I released long, thick ropes of cum on my chin, chest, and stomach. Damn, I don't remember the last time I came that much or that fast. I guess it really had been a long month in that hospital.

I gave Clark a sheepish grin and my heart skipped a beat at the look of pure desire on his face. He was frozen, standing over me with the gown clenched in his fist, his cock clearly trying to get out of his pants, his eyes looking at the cum on my body, and his mouth slightly open, tongue licking those sweet lips.

"Want some, angel?"

He blushed deeply, but nodded.

I scooped the seed off my chin with my finger and offered it to Clark. He opened his mouth and took my finger inside, sucking like it was my dick. I groaned.

"Will you undo your pants so I can touch you?"

His hands flew to his pants and he unbuttoned, then unzipped. My left arm was feeling much better and my hand was fine, so I ran my fingers over his cock and tried to get a grip on it from my angle on the bed. Frankly, it was a pretty shitty hand job, but Clark didn't seem to mind. He was moaning and tweaking my nipples.

My cock hadn't completely softened, so when my lover leaned down and sucked my balls into his mouth, I groaned and bucked up, back to full hardness immediately. Clark licked my dick like an ice cream cone, flicked his tongue on the ridge around the crown, then sucked me in to the hilt and buried his nose in my pubes.

"Yes! Oh, angel. So good."

Clark loved to give head, and he had gotten damn good at it over the years, but his technique seemed even better than I'd remembered. He was sucking hard, licking me, and swallowing around my cock as it was buried in his throat. That combination was absolutely fucking deadly and I could feel another orgasm building.

"Clark...Clark...gonna..."

I fisted the sheets with both hands, completely forgetting my mission to jack him off. I usually wasn't a selfish lover, but damn the things he was doing to me with that sweet mouth could make a man forget his name.

When he heard my warning, he pulled up so just my crown was in his willing, eager mouth, and then he dipped his tongue into my slit and squeezed my balls. That was it. I thrust my hips up, cried out his name, and poured myself into him.

I could hear Clark moaning as my seed hit his mouth, then I felt wet heat on the side of my body and realized that he had come too, without a touch. He suckled on my dick as it softened and my entire body relaxed. My toes were heavy, my fingers limp; I felt blissfully sated. Clark raised his face, licked my neck, kissed my cheek, and rested his forehead against mine as he stroked my arms and chest. We were both panting.

"Okay, it looks like I managed to make a mess on your body, rather than cleaning it. Time for that bath. I'm just going to get some warm water from the sink, because I think this basin is cold by now."

He tucked himself back into his pants, got everything

buttoned and zipped, and then rolled the cart into the bathroom. I admired how his pants draped over his ass and surprised myself by my recovery time. I'd just come twice in the past thirty minutes and my cock was making a valiant effort to pop back up at attention from the sight of Clark's firm ass. Well, it was a mighty fine ass, and my cock missed its mate. I made a mental note to ask the doctor when I was getting sprung from that hospital.

Clark was a really reserved guy. So much so that I was surprised he was willing to go down on me in the hospital. No way was he going to agree to full-on sex in that place. But if I didn't get myself inside him or him in me soon, I was sure I was going to lose my mind.

Clark—Past

"DO YOU think I might be gay?"

It was Sunday evening and my mom and I were in our living room, talking. She was sitting on the couch, with quilts covering her lap and legs, and I was lying down with my head resting on them, my legs hanging over the edge of the couch arm.

"Well, honey, I think you're the only person who can answer that question. Do you want to tell me what brought this on?"

I knew we didn't have many more evenings like that left—the two of us together, talking. The doctors had stopped trying to cure her when it became clear the treatments weren't working. On the plus side, she'd stopped throwing up every couple of hours. The downside, of course, was that every day could be her last.

"I don't know. I guess I've never been interested in girls. I hadn't thought much of it, but then last week when Ben and I went to find Noah, he said something to me."

She smoothed down my hair like she used to do when I was really little. I was probably twice her size, but she still had a calming effect on me.

"Ben said something to you?"

I closed my eyes and tried to memorize every bit of what I was feeling so I'd have the memory of my mother taking care of me to last me for the rest of my life.

"Not Ben. Noah."

"Ahh. I see. So does he feel the same way about you?"

I opened my eyes and looked up at her.

"What do you mean?"

"I mean, does Noah love you? I assume he told you that he noticed how you feel about him?"

I furrowed my brow in confusion.

"No, that's not what happened. Noah told me that he's gay. But it was like he thought I already knew. And he thinks I'm gay too. What do you mean 'how I feel about him'? How do I feel about him?"

My mom laughed softly. Damn, I was going to miss that laugh.

"Like I said, honey, only you can answer that question. But I'll tell you this—I've never seen you light up like you do when you talk about Noah. And you sure spend a lot of time with him, more time than you spend with any of your other friends."

"That's because he needs me, Mom. He needs me to drive him to his kickboxing class and he needs someone to talk to."

She gave me that "Mom" look. You know, the one where they don't say anything, but they look at you like they know you know that you just unloaded a huge pile of horseshit? Yeah, that's the one.

"Plus, I...I like spending time with him."

"Okay then."

"Okay then? What does that mean?"

"It means you have a friend who you enjoy spending time with and he enjoys being with you. It sounds like he might be interested in something more than friendship and he thinks you're open to that. And I don't hear you saying it can't happen, so, I guess you'll just have to see where it goes from here."

Now see, that was the problem with having a hippie-dippie mother. Nothing fazed her. It was as if we were discussing what to have for dinner and I asked whether she wanted garlic bread or rolls. Oh, just put them both out, honey, and we'll see where it goes from there.

"It's not going to go anywhere between me and Noah, Mom. He's only thirteen. You know that."

She hadn't said a thing about the fact that he had a dick, like it wasn't even part of the equation. Well, to her, it probably wasn't. My mother was all about open-mindedness and equality. She had grown up during the civil rights movement, protested the Vietnam War, and marched in DC for all sorts of causes. Total hippie chick, my mom. God, I loved her. So much.

"And you're only seventeen, Clark. You're responsible, intelligent, mature, and my best friend in the world. But, honey, the fact that I treat you like an adult doesn't mean you are one. You're still a baby."

I burrowed closer to my mother and pressed my head against her stomach.

"It's too big an age gap."

"Have I ever told you how old your father and I were when you were conceived?"

"You were forty and he was…"

Huh. I guess I'd never asked how old he was. I didn't ask much about him. I suppose he didn't enter my mind very often. She finished my sentence when it became clear I didn't know the answer.

"Twenty-four. I was forty and he was twenty-four. So if I'm doing my math right here, honey, the sixteen-year age gap we had was four times that of your four-year age gap with Noah. It's not about your years on this planet, it's about your souls and beings. If those connect, the ages of your vessels are irrelevant."

Oh Jesus, help me with the metaphysical speak. I loved my mother, adored her, but I'd never been able to get into the whole earth-spirit-tarot-card-reading mumbo jumbo.

"Well, that's different. You and my father were both adults, living independently. You were in the same stage of life. Noah and I aren't like that, Mom. He's still in middle school for another year, and when he goes to high school, I'll be off at college. Plus, I'll be eighteen in November. At that point, it'd be criminal for me to be with him. The age of your vessel is totally relevant to the police, Mom. They don't care about souls and beings connecting."

"Illegal? So I take it you're fantasizing about having sex with him?"

I blushed furiously.

"No! I didn't say that."

She patted my head.

"Honey, humans are sexual beings. Those feelings are normal, and there's no reason to be ashamed of having them. And it's not illegal to be friends with someone younger than you. What's illegal is sticking your poker in his fire."

I immediately flashed back to the painful birds and the bees conversation my mother had with me when I was twelve. There were no birds and no bees, but there was a banana, a condom, and a thoroughly detailed description of the male body, including ejaculation, and the female body, including a rant about how awful it was when men couldn't figure out where the clitoris was or what to do with it. She went to town on that whole "a single woman can raise a boy on her own just fine, thank you" theory with that talk. Well, it seemed like the embarrassing "pin the tongue on the clitoris" game turned out to be for nothing. I groaned inwardly, thinking back to how I first thought, then hoped, and finally prayed that she was kidding when she first suggested it. She wasn't.

"All that said, you're probably right. It's better for you to keep things platonic with Noah. But you should think long and hard about what you've got going on beneath the surface, Clark, because what matters most is learning yourself. And if you're fantasizing about having sex with another guy, that might help you answer the question you asked me."

I closed my eyes and thought about what she'd said. The fact that her words made me think about what Noah's dick felt like "beneath the surface" of his clothes, and what I could do to make it "long and hard" made me realize she was right, as always. I *did* need to figure myself out. Regardless of what would or wouldn't happen with Noah—and nothing would—I had to live with myself.

Noah had used those words to explain why he was so self-destructive. He had been having trouble living with himself, because he knew himself well enough to know he wasn't the person his parents thought he was, and he hated living the lie. I hadn't been living a lie, at least not intentionally.

For me, it was more a total lack of self-awareness. I simply hadn't thought about myself and what I wanted. Well, I'd do that. I'd focus on me, on who I was and who I wanted to become. But I'd do it later. After all, my mother wouldn't be around forever, and while I had her in my life, I'd focus on her and squirrel away all the memories I could.

CHAPTER NINE

Noah—Present

I WAS back in my hospital room after a day full of tests. It had started with yet another neurological exam and moved on to an MRI, CT, and EEG. I'd never been in so many machines or been poked and prodded so much. The problem with all the focus on my head was that they forgot about my body, which was tired and sore as hell.

"Okay, Noah. Now what I'd like to do is—"

"Dr. Garcia, with all due respect, he's had enough for today."

That was my strong partner. I leaned back into the hospital bed and closed my eyes. Clark would take care of things, I didn't need to worry.

"I understand, Mr. Lehman, of course. We're almost done. I just want to do a few more—"

"You can call me Clark and there will no more anything today. He's tired, his body must be hurting, and he needs to rest. Come back tomorrow and we'll see if he's feeling up to more testing."

I wasn't watching Clark talk to the doctor, but I could see everything in my head anyway. Clark's slender body standing tall, hands crossed across his firm chest, legs probably spread apart so he'd look more authoritative, long, thick, pink, delicious cock snaking down his left leg because, well, that was where it hung. The thought of Clark's dick caused the usual Pavlovian response in me. I groaned.

There was a short silence, and then Dr. Garcia wished us a good evening, promised to be back first thing in the morning, and left. I felt Clark's heat next to me. His lips brushed my cheek, and his hand rubbed circles on my belly.

"Mmmmm. Feels good, angel. Thank you for making him go away. Love you."

"Oh God. For so long, I thought I'd never hear those words again. I love you too, Noah. So much. I love you so damn much."

His voice was breaking and he was sniffling. My poor guy had been so worried. I opened my eyes and ran my left hand through his hair.

"I'm just fine, angel. Don't cry. My left arm is almost completely healed and my right arm is getting stronger, I can tell. They said I'll get the casts off my legs in a few days. Then I'll be good as new and we can go back to how things were before we got stuck in this hospital."

That was supposed to make him feel better, but it seemed to have the opposite effect. His sniffles turned into full-on, body-shuddering tears. I tried to change the topic.

"Clark, are you okay with work? You've been here nonstop. Do you have this much time off?"

As I asked the question, I realized I had no idea whether he still worked for the same company. Clark was a computer guru, and he got a great job right out of school working for a big company doing hardware design. He'd stayed with that company when we'd moved to EC West, after I'd graduated.

"I'm fine. I actually work for myself now. I do consulting services for a bunch of companies, and I can do a lot of it remotely. I just need Wi-Fi to work, and this hospital has it. I've been getting a lot done while you've been sleeping."

No wonder he was so emotional. Between the time he'd been spending taking care of me and the time he'd been spending keeping up with work, he probably hadn't gotten much sleep. I tugged on his hand.

"Get in here, angel."

"Wha...What?"

"Get in this bed, Clark. I need you to hold me."

"I don't want to hurt you, Noah."

"Oh come on. You know I can take a little pain. Might even like it sometimes, if you're the one dishing it out."

I waggled my eyebrows at him, trying to lighten things up, ease his tension. It worked too, because he chuckled and crawled into the empty spot I'd made in the hospital bed. I lifted my neck so he could slip his arm underneath, then I turned on my side, rested my head on his chest, put my left arm on his stomach, and cupped his balls.

I hadn't been one of those kids who slept with a stuffed bear or blanket or anything, but holding Clark's balls in my hand had become my regular sleeping position from the first night we'd slept together naked. I didn't like having the layers of pants and underwear separating me from what was mine, but we were in a hospital, so I had to make do.

"Let's take a little nap, angel. I think we could both use it."

"Oh, I'd like that. I've missed sleeping with you more than you know. I can't sleep more than a couple of hours without you. I can't tell you how tired I've been these last few...ehm, are you sure that you'll be comfortable? You need your rest, sweetheart."

"This is the most comfortable I've been since I woke up in this place. 'S good to feel your body, angel. I can't sleep without you either. And I know this bed has to be better than that chair you've been sleeping in since you got here."

He sighed and his body relaxed beneath me. I closed my eyes and immediately fell asleep, the warmth and safety of Clark's body putting me completely at peace.

Clark—Past

MY MOM died that fall, four days after my eighteenth birthday.

She'd managed to hang on long enough that I didn't have to move in with any relatives. I'd be able to stay in our apartment until I finished high school.

As it turned out, being sick was crazy expensive. My mother had health insurance, but between the deductibles, co-pays, and the treatment costs that exceeded her annual limit, she had depleted all of her savings. I'd be okay though, because she had a small life insurance policy. It was enough to get me through college, as long as I was careful with the money and maybe got a part-time job to help cover expenses.

I slept at my aunt's house for a week after my mom died. That gave my aunt time to go through our apartment and clean out the meds, get the hospital bed we'd been renting sent back, and take my mom's clothes out of the closet and toiletries out of the bathroom. I'd asked her to leave everything else. Eventually, I'd have the strength to go through my mom's letters and journals, look at old pictures. Damn, I was going to miss her.

Her funeral was beautiful. It was like the earth knew one of its believers was coming home. The normally cold November weather tempered. The sky was extra blue, scattered with white, fluffy clouds, and decorated with a double rainbow. As we stood outside and lowered her casket into the ground, the leaves on the trees danced and a light breeze sailed past me in a soft caress, drying my tears before they could make their way down my cheeks.

Lots of people came out to remember my mother that

day—her friends from childhood who still lived in Emile City, her friends from all over the country who flew in to see her, her sister and cousins, and even some of my friends, including the Formans. Noah caught my gaze as my mom was lowered into the ground. Looking into his hazel eyes gave me strength and comfort. After we buried her, everyone went back to my Aunt Shirley's house and sat around telling stories about my mother.

The Formans came by, but they left after only a few minutes. I briefly wondered whether the stories had driven them away—my mother was no wallflower, and almost all of the stories involved tales of her youth, which was spent wandering the country with different men, fighting for a variety of causes.

"Clark, are you sure you don't want to stay here with us? We have plenty of space for you, dear. The girls are happy to share a room and we can put you in Tracey's room."

Everyone had left and I was helping my Aunt Shirley clean up the last of the plates and glasses.

"Thanks, Aunt Shirley, but I want to go home. I won't turn down a home-cooked meal every now and then, though."

She patted my back. It didn't feel exactly like the pats my mom used to give me, but it'd have to do.

"There's no problem with that, Clark. You're welcome here anytime. This is home now, you hear? Don't you dare try to stay away."

I gave her a hug.

"You know I won't. Good night, Aunt Shirley."

By the time I got home, it was after ten. I sighed as I set my keys in the bowl by the door and looked around. This was it, I was alone. Well, I still had her in my heart. That wouldn't ever change.

I took a long shower and let the hot water hit my back and relieve some of my tension. That was the longest I'd stood still in days, and my exhaustion finally caught up with me. When I noticed my eyelids drooping shut, I turned off the water, wiped myself dry, and shuffled to my bedroom. I pulled on some sweatpants and a long shirt, crawled under the covers, and was about to close my eyes when I heard the doorbell ring.

What the hell? A look at the clock on my nightstand told me it was after eleven o'clock. I walked out to the living room quietly, and moved toward the front door without making any noise, in case the person out there was up to no good. A quick look through the peephole confirmed that suspicion, but not in a bad way.

I swung my door open and smiled for the first time in a week.

"Noah Forman. Should I even bother asking what you're doing out at this hour?"

Noah raised his captivating hazel eyes up to meet my blue ones and my heart stuttered. He stuffed his hands in his pockets and shifted from foot to foot. For the first time since I'd met him, Noah seemed nervous.

"I wanted to see if you were okay. I...I thought you could use some company. Can I come in?"

I stepped back and made room for him to walk past. Once he was inside, I closed and locked the door.

"Let's skip the whole, 'you're only fourteen, you shouldn't be out this late. Do your parents know you're here? Call them right now or I will' speech, okay?"

His voice was soft and his eyes were filled with tears. I wanted to wipe them away, hold him close, kiss the pout off his lips. No, no, no. Not the last one. Definitely not the last one.

"Okay."

"Do you need to talk, Clark?"

Did I? Maybe. But right then, I needed sleep more than anything else.

"I'm tired, Noah. Really tired."

He took his hand out of his pocket, twined his fingers with mine, and pulled me toward the bedroom.

"Come on."

I followed him, too exhausted to gather the self-control necessary to pull away from that warm hand that felt just right in mine.

"What are you doing?"

He walked us down the hallway.

"Which door?"

"Second one on the left."

Wait, what? Why was I letting Noah take me to my bedroom?

"Noah, this isn't a good idea."

He walked us into my room, sat on the edge of the bed, and took off his shoes. I noticed what he was wearing for the first time—a pair of old, worn sweatpants, draping over the firm rod underneath them, which made me want to touch and squeeze, and a kickboxing T-shirt that had gotten tighter as he'd gotten bigger, highlighting his defined muscles. He looked good. Really good. Once his shoes were off, he crawled up the bed, pulled down the covers, and snuggled underneath.

"Get in, Clark. I promise not to make any moves on you. You look like hell. I was worried about you during the funeral today. When was the last time you had a solid night's sleep?"

It had been so long, I couldn't answer the question. Certainly not since my mom had died, and even before then, because at the end there, she'd been so sick that she was moaning and restless all the time. There was no way I could've slept through that.

I shrugged my shoulders.

"Don't remember. Too tired, I guess."

I smiled sheepishly. Noah held his hand out to me.

"Just sleep, Clark. I promise. Get in here. I'm more cuddly than a teddy bear. I guarantee a good night's sleep or your money back."

I got into bed, put my head on the pillow, and pulled the covers over my shoulders.

"I didn't pay you any money."

Noah smiled, turned his back to me, pushed himself against my chest, and rested his head on my pillow.

"Huh. Good point. Oh well. Good night, Clark. I love you."

"Noah."

My voice held a clear warning tone.

"Don't 'Noah' me. I'm fourteen, not an amphibian. I know what I'm feeling. I get that you don't want to hear it, that it makes you uncomfortable, or whatever. But that doesn't mean it isn't true. I won't say it again, but it's *true*. Now close your eyes and go to sleep."

Incredibly, I did. For the first time in as long as I could remember, I slept well and soundly through the night. And I held Noah Forman in my arms the entire time.

CHAPTER TEN

Noah—Present

"WHAT I'M saying is that the issue doesn't seem to be physical."

I had finally gotten the casts removed from both of my legs. I was just barely starting to regain the full use of my right arm. My body was covered in yellowing bruises. How in the hell was all that not physical?

"Work with me here, Dr. Garcia. I have no idea what you mean."

"Noah, I've done every test imaginable and I can't find any reason for your memory loss. My best guess is that this is a post-traumatic stress type of reaction."

Of course, he was talking about the memory loss. The internist and the nurses had been dealing with my physical injuries. Dr. Garcia's interest had been almost exclusively focused on my brain. I thought about what he'd said. I couldn't remember anything from the past three years because of some mental block?

"What, like because of the accident, you mean? I'm

stressed about the accident so I can't remember?"

Dr. Garcia nodded.

"Well, that's certainly part of it. It might be all of it. Hard to say, really. What's unusual here is that you're having no trouble with short-term memory. You seem to remember everything that happened from the moment you woke up. And your long-term memory is excellent too, up until a specific date. Then it's a blank slate. Now if that date correlated with your accident, it wouldn't be so unusual. But we're talking about three years here, and there's no physical reason for you to have a gap like that."

Clark's hand was in mine, so I could feel when it clenched. I looked at him and immediately became concerned. All the color had drained from his face. He was completely white and looked like he was about to throw up.

"Angel? You okay?"

"I... Yes... No... Uh..."

He turned to the doctor.

"What could cause that? I mean, could the post-traumatic stress thing happen from another stressful event? One from back then? Back when he stopped remembering?"

Dr. Garcia shrugged.

"That's certainly possible. The brain is a complicated organ. We're learning new things every day, but in the scheme of things, we don't know much about how it reacts to trauma, whether physical or emotional."

Dr. Garcia got up to leave the room.

"It's very possible that it will all come back to you, Noah. Maybe when you go home tomorrow, something will spark your memory."

I imagine that my smile took over my entire face.

"I'm getting out of here tomorrow?"

I beamed at Clark.

"Did you hear that, angel? We're going home!"

Dr. Garcia chuckled.

"Don't act so surprised. That's what you've been pestering me and the entire staff about for days. Your body is doing much better. Your physical therapist told me he's never seen anyone recover so quickly, and he's afraid you're going to drop-kick him if you don't get out of here. With Clark's help, there's no reason you can't go home. You need to take it easy, of course. No strenuous exercise and lots of sleep. At least for a few more weeks."

I nodded furiously. We could finally go home and sleep in our bed. And do other things in that bed too. And on the couch. Oh, and the shower would be good too. Home.

Clark—Past

THE NEXT week was strange. It was hard to deal with the reality of coming home and not seeing my mom's smile greet me, going to sleep without her good-night kiss to warm me, and waking up without hearing her voice. Whenever I got too down, I'd pull out one of our old photo albums and flip through the pictures. That was always enough to bring a smile to my face.

I had Thanksgiving dinner with my aunt and uncle's family and got back to my apartment at eight that night with four grocery bags overflowing with leftovers. I'd tried to explain to my aunt that it was anatomically impossible for me to consume that quantity of food before it'd spoil, but she kept mumbling something about growing boys while she stuffed the bags as full as she could. Eventually, I'd decided going along with the madness was easier than arguing with her.

As I approached my apartment, I noticed a figure sitting on the floor, slumped against the door. When I got closer, I saw the green Mohawk. My dick immediately perked up and tried to wave hello. I gave myself an internal reprimand and reminder of our four-year age gap, then tapped his foot with mine. Noah's head popped up from where it had been resting on his folded hands.

"Happy Thanksgiving. To what do I owe the honor?"

"Did you mean it when you said you'd help me?"

His voice sounded so tired and despondent.

"Of course I did, Noah. Come inside. I'll see if I can rustle up something for us to eat."

I looked down at the bags in my arms as I spoke and

rolled my eyes. Noah stood and brushed off his pants. He had grown a couple inches since I'd met him, so he was just a few inches shorter than me. He peered into the bags and smiled.

"That looks good. I'm so hungry! Haven't eaten all day."

I frowned, wondering why he hadn't eaten on Thanksgiving, and handed him two of the bags so I could get my keys out of my pocket. As soon as we made it into the apartment, I unloaded the food and heated up an overflowing plate for Noah. He had seconds, a piece of pumpkin pie, and a piece of pecan pie. I shook my head at him and smiled. He giggled and rubbed his hand across his flat stomach.

"I'm a growing boy."

He was so adorable he made my chest hurt.

"My Aunt Shirley must be a fortune teller or something."

"What?"

He had one eyebrow raised and a quizzical expression on his intriguing face.

"She kept going on about growing boys when she packed this food. Doesn't matter."

I waved my hand in the air, indicating a change of topic.

"I like the hair. When did you get it done?"

He snickered and a devilish look took over his features.

"Right after my father complained about the length of my hair and said I needed a haircut. Careful what you wish for, Pop!"

He toasted his father silently and finished his glass of water. I sat across from him, propped my elbows on the table, and rested my head in my hands.

"What's going on, Noah?"

He pushed the empty plate away and sighed.

"Today was totally fucked. We were all supposed to go to my grandparents' house for dinner. My parents were fluttering all around us, wanting us to look just so. Then my father mentioned that one of my cousins was bringing her roommate with her. I could tell from the tone of his voice and the look of horror on my mother's face that the roommate isn't just a roommate, you know? My mother complained about how 'that' wasn't appropriate in front of children. Then she called my aunt to tell her she shouldn't allow her daughter's roommate to come to our family dinner because she isn't family. I don't know what my aunt said, but based on my mom's attitude, it was clear my cousin and her girlfriend were still coming.

"The entire time this was going on, Ben sat on the couch, flipping through a magazine, like it was all perfectly normal. I'm telling you, Clark, there's no way I could have sat through that meal watching my cousin endure my parents without taking someone's eye out with a fork. So I picked a fight, stormed to my bedroom, and refused to open the door when they knocked. Eventually, they left without me, no doubt after weighing which would be more socially appropriate—

being late or coming with one less person."

He was twisting his fingers and cracking his knuckles while he spoke. I reached across the table and took his hand in between both of mine.

"Have I told you how proud I am of you?"

I thought he'd make a snide remark, but he didn't. He just gave me a soft, heart-wrenching smile.

"You haven't used since that day we talked, have you?"

He shook his head.

"I promised you I wouldn't, so I haven't. But what am I going to do, Clark? I can't take much more of this. Something has to give."

I got up, walked over to the table by the front door, and returned with an envelope.

"One of my mom's old friends is the dean of a boarding school back East. He was at the funeral and I talked to him about you."

I handed him the envelope with the enrollment application and literature about the school.

"It's very exclusive and well-known. The kind of place your parents would love to brag about to all their friends. And the best part is, you can be yourself there—no more hiding. The dean is very open-minded, they have a gay-straight alliance, and he promised me nobody there would tell your parents about your personal life. You have a spot if you want it, Noah."

He looked surprised and confused.

"But I'd have to be away from you if I go there. I...I don't want that."

Oh Noah. That boy had a way of breaking my heart without even trying. I squeezed his hand.

"There are phones. We can talk as often as you want. Besides, this is probably for the best. The older you get, the more I worry about my ability to resist your charms."

I chuckled until I saw Noah's smoldering look.

"Yeah?"

I cleared my throat, pulled back my hand, and shifted uncomfortably in my seat.

"Stop, Clark. Don't close yourself off from me. It's a simple question. Is the whole jailbait issue the only thing standing in our way, or are you not interested in me because I'm like a bottomless pit of emotional needs? The *truth*, Clark. You're the only person I can trust, don't you dare take that away from me because you're scared."

And therein lay the problem with resisting Noah. He didn't sound like any fourteen-year-old I'd ever met. I had to constantly remind my dick that he was too young, so it'd stand down and not embarrass me. Hell, it wasn't just my dick. My entire body practically shook with the need to wrap around him, touch him, smell him, taste him.

"I think it's safe to say that I am *very* interested in you, Noah. But you really are too young for me, so nothing can happen between us."

He looked determined.

"For now."

Some tension left my body with the thought that someday I could actually stop holding myself back.

"Yeah. For now."

NOAH APPLIED to the boarding school and then showed his parents the acceptance letter. They were thrilled. Saying they were just happy about their son going to a fancy school they could brag about to their friends wouldn't be fair. The truth was, the Formans loved Noah and they were worried about him. He had been spiraling out of control, there was nothing they could do to stop him, and he created a palpable air of tension in their house. The thought of him going to a place where he would study and behave gave them hope for his future. They really did want the best for their son.

The school started in grade six, but Noah was going to be in grade nine. He wouldn't be the only new kid and he had no trouble making friends, so he wasn't worried. Still, he used the whole "missed the first three years" as an excuse to explain why he wanted to go to the summer session. Something about getting to know people and getting used to the campus before everyone else got there. But the truth was, he was desperate to get the hell out of Dodge.

So that May, Noah finished middle school, Ben and I graduated from high school, and all of our lives moved in new directions. Noah's flight back East was early Monday morning, a week after graduation. Sunday night, he showed up at my door. I wasn't surprised.

"I know the drill, Clark. But I'll be gone for four years. Will you just hold me tonight? Just spooning, no forking."

By that point in time, I'd probably have given him anything he wanted. I was devastated that he was no longer going to be a regular part of my life. But his earnest, almost-begging voice was what did me in. I simply couldn't lie to myself about my feelings for Noah in light of the way my body automatically reacted to him. There was no other way to explain the persistent, aching hard-ons.

I didn't tell him, of course, because I knew it wouldn't be good for him. But my heart hurt with the knowledge that we'd be so far apart, and with the certainty that he'd move on from his little crush on me. There'd be other guys at his new school—good guys, smart guys—and he'd realize I was nothing special.

So I held him in my arms that night, knowing it'd probably be the last time. It was all I could do to hold back the tears accompanying that realization. I wrapped myself around him and he snuggled against my chest, tucked one leg between both of mine, and pressed his body firmly against my side.

"Someday we'll sleep like this every night."

I didn't say anything, because I knew by the time someday came, he'd have moved on from me. The thought alone was enough to twist my stomach in knots. I didn't know if he was reading my mind, just knew me really well, or could feel my body tense, but Noah rubbed his hand over my belly and mumbled into my neck.

"You'll see, Clark. I'll be back in four years and we're going to start living our lives. Just please don't have someone else in my bed then. When I get back, I'll be coming home to you and anyone standing in my way isn't going to be standing for long."

I chuckled and rubbed his back.

"Okay, tough guy."

He lifted his head off my chest and looked into my eyes.

"I'm only tough with other people. Not with you, Clark. I'll never, ever hurt you."

I knew that he could, of course. He was shorter than me, but much stronger and rougher. Frankly, Noah could have taken anyone down in a fight, but I'd never known anybody dumb enough to test that theory. Besides, putting physical strength aside, Noah Forman had me completely wrapped around his little finger.

"I know you won't hurt me, Noah. I know."

CHAPTER ELEVEN

Noah—Present

"NOAH, WE need to talk about something Dr. Garcia said."

Clark was lying next to me on the hospital bed. His arm was snaked behind my head and he was stroking my hair. I had my head on his chest, one hand rubbing his balls, and the other holding his hand.

"Did he ask you why you need to give me two sponge baths every day? It's about time folks around here started wondering about the reason for that."

He snickered.

"I don't think they're wondering about the reason, sweetheart. The hospital walls aren't that thick and you don't know how to keep it down in the sack. Thank God."

"Yeah? You like the noises you bring out of me, angel?"

My voice was husky and low and I was stroking his dick.

"Jesus, Noah."

He was breathing hard, eyes closed.

"I really want to talk to you. Can't do that when you're

getting me all hot and bothered."

I reluctantly moved my hand, then kissed his neck.

"Okay, angel. What are we talking about?"

There was a long silence, and when I looked at Clark's face, I could see that he was scared.

"What's wrong, Clark?"

He cleared his throat and answered me in a whisper.

"I don't ever want to be away from you again. Don't leave me, Noah. Please. Just give me a chance."

What the hell? I looked deep into those frightened eyes.

"Angel, what are you saying? I'll *never* leave you. Count on that, okay? What's going on?"

He closed his eyes, then answered me.

"I know what happened on December 27th, 2007. You know, the first day you don't remember? I know what happened."

My chest tightened in a "someone just dropped a one-hundred pound weight on it" kind of way. I didn't like the sound of his voice, and I suspected I wouldn't feel any better once I heard what he was about to tell me, but I didn't say anything. He continued talking, with his peepers still closed and his forehead furrowed in concentration.

"The doctor said there's no physical reason for your memory loss, that maybe it's because of something from back then."

"You're scaring me, Clark. I don't think I want to know

this. Let's just leave the past where it is and go back to our regular lives."

He made a strange, strangled sound, almost like a sob, then opened his crystal-blue eyes and looked into mine.

"I need to tell you what happened, Noah. We have to clear the air before you're released tomorrow. It's the only way for us to lead the lives I know we both want."

I braced myself. I could take it. Whatever it was, I could take it. I could handle anything as long as I had Clark.

"Okay. Tell me."

A firm kiss to the top of my head, a squeeze to my hand, then Clark started talking with a shaky voice.

"We had just closed on the bungalow in EC West, but we hadn't moved in yet because there was so much to fix up that we thought it'd make more sense to stay in our apartment."

So far, so good. I remembered all of that, so I nodded.

"The morning of the twenty-seventh, we got a call from the lady who lived next door to the new house and she said there was a lot of water around the foundation. We got up to go over there. Then your brother called."

That was new. I hadn't remembered having a conversation with my brother in over two years. But as Clark spoke, I started seeing it in my mind, the memories floating back in.

"Ben was upset. Really upset. You hadn't seen him in so long and he wanted to talk with you. We hoped he was finally ready to make up, so I went to the house and you went to see your brother. I thought everything was fine between us."

Something hurt in my chest, but I didn't know why. Oh God. It was coming back to me. Slowly coming back to me.

"I couldn't get a hold of you after that. You didn't answer your cell and I didn't know where you were. I was so worried. I took care of the broken pipe at the house, went back to our apartment, got cleaned up, and went looking for you."

No. No. Please no.

"I couldn't find you anywhere. Not at our friends' houses, not at the pizza place down the street you liked so much, not at the coffee shop on the corner. Eventually I started searching bars and calling hospitals, but that didn't work either. I was scared to death, I didn't know where else to look, and you weren't answering your phone."

I clutched Clark's chest so hard that my nails dug into his skin, sure to leave marks. My heart was in my throat and my eyes were open wide in horror.

"It was late by then, almost midnight. I went back to our apartment, figuring the only thing left to do was to call your brother."

Oh God. The memories from that night assaulted me in one huge wave of regret and pain. What had I done?

"You were sitting on the armchair in the living room, that old plaid one we got from your grandmother. There was a guy I didn't recognize with you and he…he was on his knees in front of you with…"

He was crying now. My angel was barely able to get the words out. I wanted to stop him. It had all come back to me. That night and every night since. Every miserable moment of the past three years was back in my head. If only I could find a way to change it. But I couldn't. Hell, I couldn't even open my mouth to tell my angel to stop talking and reliving that awful night.

"He had your dick in his mouth, and when you heard me come in, you just…you looked at me. Just looked at me standing there and didn't say anything."

That was the worst night of my life. The devastation in Clark's gorgeous face. I broke him that night. Sure as I could see the tears in his eyes, I could see that. I loved him more than anything, and I broke him.

"I'm so sorry, angel. I was such a stupid jerk. Forgive me, Clark. Please forgive me."

He shook underneath me. I rolled on top of him and wrapped my arms around him so all he could feel was my weight, my heat, surrounding him.

"Will you forgive me, Noah?"

"For what, angel? It was me. You didn't do anything wrong."

"Oh yes, I did. I gave up on us and walked away. I was such an idiot, Noah. But I know that now and it won't happen again. I'll always fight for us. Just give me one more chance."

Those were words I'd never expected to hear. Not words I'd deserved to hear. I was the one who'd made the mistake. I was the one who'd broken our promises. I was the one who'd broken his heart.

"Angel, I just want you back. I know you're only here because I'm in this hospital, but I'm not too proud to take it. I'll take you any way I can get you, Clark, even if it's for pity. But I'll show you that I won't hurt you again. I'll remind you about how good we are together. And I know you'll decide to stay, even when I'm recovered."

It was hard to tell his tears from mine; our faces were pressed together, both of us crying, hands holding each other's cheeks.

"I'll stay forever this time, Noah. Just like I always said I would. I don't want to leave. And it has nothing to do with your injuries. I'd been living in LA, you know. I couldn't have gotten to this hospital so fast if that were still the case."

"What? I don't understand."

"I moved back, sweetheart. I finally realized what an ass I've been all these years, so I packed a bag and came home. I planned to woo you, win you back. But I hadn't even been here long enough to find a hotel when my phone rang and it was my aunt, saying the hospital found her number on an old emergency contact form for me. They told her you were hurt and you wanted to see me."

I had to laugh. Just had to.

"Woo me back? I've been waiting for you. I knew you'd

eventually come home to me. I've been waiting all this time. No wooing necessary. I'm yours, Clark. Always have been, always will be. Yours. Just *yours*."

Clark—Past

I DROVE Noah to his parents' house early the morning after he snuck over to my apartment. That way, he could sneak into his room before the rest of the family woke up to take him to the airport and out of my life. We said our goodbyes, promised to keep in touch with frequent phone calls and e-mails, and then sat in the front seat of my car and stared at each other.

I saw need and hope and, yes, maybe even love in his eyes, but I wasn't sure whether that was just a reflection of my feelings for him. I hoped not. I hoped more than anything that his feelings for me were real and that they'd still be there when he finished high school.

"Aw, fuck it," I muttered as I leaned over the console, wrapped my hand around the back of Noah's head, and pulled him toward me for a kiss.

He whimpered and melted against me, his entire body pliant, yielding to my touch; so different from the tense, confrontational guy he showed the rest of the world. His lips were soft and warm and we enjoyed a tender caress of lips and tongue before I finally forced myself to pull away.

"Four years."

Noah panted as he reached his arm behind his back and opened the car door. Then he scooted backward out of the car, raised his hand in a silent goodbye, and walked to his parents' house.

THE NEXT four years passed by without me ever seeing Noah. He managed to find an excuse to skip a trip home for every vacation: summer school, trip abroad, vacation with friends, kickboxing tournament, etc., etc., etc. Mr. and Mrs. Forman spent a weekend here and there visiting him. From what Ben told me when he'd occasionally join them on those trips, Noah was busy and had very little time to spend with them. Of course I knew the truth—he simply didn't want to be around his family, so he came up with every reason possible to avoid them.

The Formans were sad, because they missed him, but they were thrilled with how well he was doing in school. I think everyone other than me expected disciplinary issues and possible expulsion during the first week he spent there, but it never happened. The truth was, Noah wasn't going to do anything that could result in having to live with his parents again.

So Noah stayed in boarding school across the country,

and I stayed in Emile City for college. Going to State cost less money than private colleges and out-of-state universities, so I was able to spread my mom's life insurance further.

For some reason I didn't understand at the time, Ben decided to go to State too. He got offers at tons of great schools all over the country and his parents had plenty of money to pay for any of them, but he stayed at State. We roomed together for all four years—first in the dorm and then in the frat house.

Ben was a wonderful friend and a fun roommate. We spent most of our free time together, made a good group of friends with some other guys from our frat, and even took some of the same classes. The only thing we never did together was double-date.

That man went through girlfriends like water. I'd barely register his latest girl's name before he'd be on to the next one. And it seemed like every girl had a friend or relative whom she wanted to set up with me.

Now that sounded like I was dancing on the head of a pin, but I didn't feel like I was hiding my orientation, even though I never told my friends that I was gay. In my mind, it didn't matter because I hadn't met a guy I wanted to date. Of course, I knew I'd probably never meet that guy because I was hopelessly hung up on Noah. The highlight of my week was talking to him on the phone. But that wasn't information I could share with anyone for lots of reasons, not the least of which was the fact that Noah didn't want his family to know he was gay.

Anyway, I never told Ben or his girlfriends that I wasn't interested in girls in general, but I always refused the setups they offered. Then one night, Ben's latest girl threw me for a loop. It was a Saturday night during our junior year and I'd stayed late at the library, studying. I was majoring in computer engineering, so I spent many a weekend night with my books and laptop. Anyway, the lights were off when I got back to our room. I assumed Ben was out with his latest girlfriend—Cheryl or maybe Cheri. Whatever.

I opened the door, dropped my backpack on the desk next to it, and flipped on the light. That was when I heard the groan and looked over at the beds. Ben was in his bed with a very naked Cheryl/Cheri. I blushed deeply.

"Shit. Sorry, Ben. I didn't realize you were in here. I'll just take off for a little while."

The girl's high voice wafted over.

"You don't have to leave, Clark. You're welcome to join us."

My jaw dropped open and I stared back at What's-her-name. She had some nerve propositioning another guy with her boyfriend right next to her, hell, possibly inside her for all I knew. Remarkably, Ben seemed unfazed. I wondered if he was drunk.

"Umm. Yeah. I don't think Ben would appreciate that, Cher...ehm, I'll just leave you to it."

Ben weighed in on the discussion.

"I don't mind, Clark. You can join us."

Okay, now that was even more surprising. Ben was a super-generous guy. He'd often offer to buy me dinner, spring for trips, stuff like that. I never let him, even though his parents gave him a credit card with no limit. I had enough to get by and that was all I needed. Anyway, this took generosity to a whole new—and strange—level.

"I'm good, Ben. Thanks."

And with those parting words, I got out of that room so fast I thought there might be a Road Runner cartoon-like trail behind me. What in the hell was that?

CHAPTER TWELVE

Noah—Present

CLARK PULLED into the driveway of our bungalow and blinked his eyes in surprise.

"It's...beautiful. It looks just like how we planned."

When we bought the house, the pink paint was peeling off, half the shutters were missing, the windows were cracked, and the shingles on the roof were rotting. You can imagine my surprise when Clark said he wanted us to make a purchase offer. It was affordable, true enough. But it was also a shithole. He had a vision, though, and he told me all about it in excruciating detail when we walked through the house. So I'd agreed to buy it. Not because I saw the vision, but because that was what he'd wanted.

"I remembered every word, angel. White paint, black shutters, wood windows, gray shingles, red door. I wasn't sure about the plants, because you just said lots of flowers and shrubs, but I hope you approve."

He nodded, clearly speechless.

"It's perfect, Noah. Perfect. Let's get inside. It's too

cold for you to be sitting out here."

He got out of the car, came around to my door, and helped me out. I was doing much better; my legs were a little stiff, nothing some stretching and a few crescent kicks wouldn't resolve. So I could manage on my own, but why turn away a chance to press my body against Clark's? I'm not stupid.

"Here, sweetheart. Lean on the car for one sec while I get my bag out of the trunk."

He tenderly set me against the side of the car, quickly opened the trunk, slung his duffel over one shoulder, and then wrapped his free arm around my waist. I leaned on him as we walked up the sidewalk and onto the front porch. I could feel the hard planes of his body and his long, lean muscles working underneath his shirt.

"You're stronger, more muscular."

He blushed and squeezed my waist.

"Not like you, but yeah. I've been working out a lot these past few years."

A painful feeling flooded my stomach and my heart clenched. I swallowed hard and asked the question that entered my mind, even though I already knew the answer. I *knew*.

"Why? Were you on the prowl or something? Hoping to find a new boyfriend?"

Clark's reaction was so sharp and sudden, that I almost lost my footing. He dropped his bag, turned so we were face-to-face, grasped my shoulders, and looked into my eyes with a fierce glare.

"Never. I *never* wanted another boyfriend. My heart is yours. I promised you that, Noah. I promised *us* that, and no pain on earth was going to change it. There were a couple of if-he-can-be-with-other-guys-so-can-I blow jobs when I first moved away. But that phase didn't last. If I couldn't be with you, I'd be alone. Nobody could ever take your place. Tell me you get that."

His grasp on my shoulders was stronger now, fingers digging in deep enough to leave bruises. Jesus, fuck, that turned me on. The passion, the possession, the pain. It made me so hot I was able to hear that he had touched other guys without demanding their names, finding them, and tearing their dicks off on the spot.

"Tell me, Noah. Say you understand that I have always been yours. Even when I was gone. Even when we were apart. Say it."

I growled, wrapped my fingers in his hair, and pulled his face to mine for a bruising kiss. Our lips met, tongues licked, teeth clicked. I moved my head to the side to change the angle, and there, there, we were pressed so tight together that I could taste blood from lips hitting teeth. Didn't matter. He moaned, I groaned, and then I pushed my tongue in and out of his mouth, showing him exactly what we'd be doing when we finally got out of the front yard and into the house.

When the need for oxygen became so overwhelming

I thought we'd both pass out, I pulled my mouth back and tugged at his hair so he'd raise his eyes to mine.

"I know you're mine, Clark. I've always known. Even when you were away, angel. I knew. You belong to me."

"Good."

Bag back over his shoulder, arm around my waist, he walked us to the door and reached into his pocket for his keys. The kiss had caused a haze in my mind, but I couldn't help noticing the fact that he had kept our house key on his key chain. When he opened the door, that thought cleared and I held my breath in anticipation.

"Oh my God."

He stood in the entryway and looked around. Refinished wood floors, all the paint removed from the woodwork so it was back to its natural state, a soft yellow color on the walls, and a stripped-down brick fireplace flanked by built-in bookcases.

"Noah, it's perfect. It's just like how I saw it in my head. How did you do all of this?"

He ran his hands over the original woodwork.

"I've had lots of free nights and weekends over the past few years. It took months to get the layers of paint off the wood because I had to do it by hand, so it wouldn't be ruined. I'm glad you like it."

When I hadn't been working, I'd spent my time on home repairs. I owned a small kickboxing gym. After my talk with Clark at the hospital, I called over there, half expecting to hear a message saying the line had been disconnected, but my friend and employee Kelsey had kept it going. Thank goodness for her and the automatic payment plan on my bills.

"Come in here." I pulled Clark into the kitchen and showed him the black and white tiles on the floor, the white subway tiles on the wall, and the white marble counters.

"You remembered."

He was walking around almost reverently, taking in all the details.

"Of course I remembered. You told me what our home would look like. I couldn't possibly forget that."

I showed him the laundry room, dining room, hall bathroom, and side bedroom. He had the same reaction in every room—a gasp, a smile, and amazement that I'd remembered which walls to take down, which light fixtures to replace, and every single wall color. I was feeling pretty proud of myself. And then I led him into the master suite.

"I took out the wall between this room, the one next to it, and the attached bathroom. And, just like you said, there was enough room for a nice bathroom, a walk-in closet, and a small study."

Clark looked amazed and happy. But when he walked into the closet, tears filled his eyes.

"Those are my clothes."

They were hanging in the closet, right next to mine. After he'd left that awful night, three years earlier, he'd never come back, never called, never wrote, never asked for his things. He'd just changed his number and disappeared from my life.

I stepped up behind him, pressed my chest against his back, wrapped my arms around his firm, flat belly, and rested my chin on his shoulder.

"Yes, they're your clothes. And they're hanging in our closet. Just like your toothbrush is sitting in a cup in our bathroom and that shampoo you like so much is in our shower. This is our home. Don't think that you taking a little trip was going to change that. I've been waiting, Clark. Waiting for you to come home."

Clark—Past

DURING THE fall of our senior year, Ben applied to graduate schools. I came home one day and found him sitting at his desk, reading a letter. I walked by him and ruffled his hair before I sat down at the end of the couch.

"What's up, bro?"

He glanced up at me, chewed on his bottom lip, then dropped the letter on the desk, and joined me on the couch. He sat down right next to me so that our sides were pressed together, but he didn't meet my eyes. He stared down at his lap and chewed on his fingernail.

"I got into the University of Chicago."

I tried to twist my body so I could give him a hug.

"That's great, Ben! Isn't that one of the best law schools in the country? You must be thrilled!"

Ben had always been so happy, the life of the party. Other than his concerns over his brother, nothing ever got Ben down. And I'd never seen him nervous. Until that day.

"Oh, umm, yeah. I guess. You're staying here, right?"

I had gotten into a 3/2 program at State. Basically, I'd spend five years instead of four and graduate with a BS and a master's.

"Yup. One more year."

"I got into the law school here too. I could stay."

I laughed and patted his leg as I tried to squeeze myself off the couch.

"Of course you got in here. You're brilliant. But you're going to leave these yahoos in the dust. And Chicago will be awesome. Let's go celebrate, brother."

He clasped my arm. When I looked at him in surprise, I couldn't recognize what I saw in his eyes.

"We're not actually brothers, Clark. Do you really think I should go to Chicago?"

I shook his arm off, feeling uncharacteristically uncomfortable with my best friend all of a sudden.

"Well, you're the closest thing to a brother I've ever had, dickweed. And of course you should go. It's a great program and you'll love living in that city. Come on, let's get the gang together and go out to celebrate. I'll even spring for the first round of redheaded sluts at the bar."

It's a drink, people. Of course with Ben, it was possible he'd meet a redhead at the bar and add her to his ever-growing list of ex-girlfriends, but that wasn't what I meant.

I WAS lucky to have early finals that year, so I had time to move my things out of the frat house and into an apartment before graduation. I'd still be going to school at State for another year, but I wasn't going to be an active member in the fraternity—four years was plenty long enough. Most of my friends were moving away, anyway—to grad schools, their hometowns, or jobs in other parts of the state.

Ben went back to his parents' house right after graduation. He was going to hang out there for a few days, do some shopping, and then spend the summer traveling through Europe before starting grad school. He'd tried to talk me into joining him, but I'd passed. I told him it was because I didn't have the money, and I refused his offer to fund the trip. That was all true. I wasn't exactly rolling in dough. But the major thing holding me back was my hope that I'd get to see Noah.

He'd finished high school the same week Ben had graduated. We still had our weekly telephone calls, and we wrote to each other all the time, but Noah hadn't told me what he was going to do now that he was done with high school, and I hadn't wanted to ask. I wasn't sure whether that was because I didn't want to make him feel any sense of obligation to follow through on the promise he'd made me four years earlier, or because I didn't want to hear him say out loud what I'd always known—that he'd moved on and was no longer interested in me.

My aunt had put all of my mom's furniture, dishes, and other household items in storage when I moved to school. The weekend after Ben's graduation, my uncle showed up in a rented moving van loaded with all of those things. I got a couple of my buddies who hadn't moved away yet to help out, and by that evening, we'd unloaded the truck into my new apartment.

My uncle took me out to dinner and then set off for the hour-long drive back to the suburbs. I'd just finished making the bed, and was trying to decide whether I should unpack the boxes holding the kitchen supplies, when I heard a knock on the door. I carefully stepped over the boxes and the rest of the stuff scattered on the floor, and made my way to the door.

When the door swung open, I had to raise my blue eyes to meet his hazel ones. He was about six feet five inches tall, and his broad shoulders looked even more imposing than they had when he was a kid. He wore orange sneakers, frayed canvas pants, and a long-sleeved green henley over a white T-shirt. He had fabric and leather bracelets lining both wrists and a leather braid around his neck holding a disk with a yin/yang symbol painted on it. His brown hair was long, with lighter streaks in it from time spent in the sun. He had a shadow on his face that wasn't quite a beard, more like he hadn't shaved in a couple of days. And he held the largest duffel bag I'd ever seen.

My mouth went dry, my heart raced, and my dick got hard so fast it ached. Noah.

CHAPTER THIRTEEN

Noah—Present

CLARK BOWED his head, and I could feel a shiver run through his body before his shoulders began shaking. I turned him to me.

"No more tears. We're home now. Everything is okay."

I couldn't talk after that because my mouth was covered with Clark's.

"Missed you so damn much, Noah."

His words were mumbled and spoken into my mouth as he walked me backward out of the closet. I felt the bed hit the back of my knees. Clark's warm hands took hold of the bottom of my sweatshirt and pulled it over my head, taking the T-shirt I wore underneath with it.

I moaned with excitement and pushed my dick against his.

"Fuck, yes, Clark."

My pants were next—button, zipper, then a push down to my feet, where Clark was squatting. He unlaced my shoes, took them off, and got rid of the socks and the jeans bunched at my ankles. Once I was naked, Clark looked over my shoulder at the bed.

"That's our bed."

I reached for his sweater and tried to pull it over his head, but my arms and shoulders were still sore, so my range of motion was a bit limited. Clark took over and got rid of his clothes. Damn, that man's dick was something spectacular. Long and thick, it bobbed up and jutted straight out from his body. Just as mouthwatering were his big, low-hanging balls. I couldn't decide which I wanted to lick and suck first.

"Of course it's our bed. You know how much I love it. I don't think I can spread my arms enough yet for you to tie me to the posts at the ends of the bed, but I'm sure we can figure something out with the slats on top."

Clark nuzzled my neck.

"Anything you need, sweetheart. You know that, right? I'll give you anything you need, Noah."

I had always had a darker side to me than Clark. He knew that, of course, because it was the reason we had any kink at all in our sex life. I'd always realized that, unlike me, Clark would have been perfectly satisfied with a vanilla sex life. And it wasn't like I didn't enjoy the vanilla. I enjoyed every moment with him. But I also wanted something else— not something more or less, just something else to add to the mix.

We'd played around with it from time to time during the course of our relationship, but I'd never wanted to push him too far. Over the three years that we'd been apart, though, I'd learned a lot more. Not that I'd fooled around with other guys. But all those nights alone left a lot of time for porn. And I definitely gravitated toward a certain type of porn. Now that he was back, there were some fantasies I wanted to explore. Not right away, but damn soon.

"Let's get in bed."

Clark walked us over to the side of the bed, shoved the comforter aside, and eased me down onto the cool sheets. Then he got in, pulled the blanket over us, and straddled my waist.

His mouth found mine again and we kissed passionately. It felt so good and so right to be with him again, to have him in our home and in our bed. I thrust my dick up against his.

"I want you, Clark. I need you so much."

I could feel his hard cock leaving a wet trail against my hip. My ass clenched in response.

"I want you too, Noah. But your body isn't healed enough yet. I'm not sure what we can do."

I groaned with disappointment. Maybe my muscles needed to be stretched before I could take part in seriously acrobatic lovemaking. But even though getting on my hands and knees or having my legs pinned over my body like I enjoyed probably wouldn't be the most comfortable things in the world, they weren't out of the question, and I was horny as hell.

Clark's hand was soft and gentle on my cheek.

"Noah?"

I looked into his warm, caring eyes.

"Yeah?"

"I've had a lot of time to think over the past few years, about us, about you, about what I think turns you on. You can tell me no, okay. It's fine and I promise that we'll take care of this."

He stroked my cock in his gentle hand as he spoke. I moaned. I'd do anything he wanted.

"What am I saying no to?"

"Do you want me to fuck your face, Noah?"

Oh Jesus! My cock pulsed in his hand, my eyes rolled back in my head, and I stopped breathing. The words and the idea of Clark doing that to me were so damn erotic that I couldn't speak. I just nodded.

"I can do that, Noah. I can give you what you need."

He sat up and dragged me to the end of the bed. I was lying on my back with my head hanging over the edge of the mattress. Clark squatted down on the floor so his face was next to mine, he put one hand under my head, and he spoke quietly into my ear while he petted my chest with his gentle touch.

"I'm going to take you now, Noah. I'm going to put my cock in your mouth and I'm not going to stop until I'm ready. Your job is to lie here and take it. Do you understand?"

His voice and touch were the same as always, calm,

kind, and gentle. But there was an iron strength in his tone that was new in the context of our lovemaking. That, combined with his description of how he planned to dominate me, was enough to make me come. Clark must have realized where things were heading, because his eyes snapped up toward my body and then he wrapped his hand around the base of my dick and squeezed.

"Correction. You have two jobs. Lie here and accept my cock in your mouth and in your throat. And don't come, Noah."

The pressure he was putting around my dick increased.

"Do we understand each other?"

I had closed my eyes, but I opened them in response to his question and searched his blue gaze. Still my Clark, my angel. But oh my fuck, he had gotten even hotter.

"Answer me, Noah. Do you understand that you cannot, you *will* not, come? Not until I give you permission."

At that point my vocal cords made a noise I'd never before heard. It was a whimper, a moan, a prayer, and a grateful sigh all wrapped into one. I swallowed hard and croaked out my answer.

"I understand."

I hesitated then, not sure whether he'd be okay with what I had to say, but it was all so close to my fantasies that I had to continue. I looked into his eyes and unleashed my desires.

"Thank you, sir."

I was half-worried I'd repulse him with that statement, but he didn't even flinch. He just stroked my hair and kissed my cheek.

"I'm glad we understand each other, Noah."

And with those words, he stood and removed the hand that had been cupping the back of my head, keeping it elevated. He ran his hands down my arms until they reached my wrists, then he held me in place. When I couldn't move, he straddled my head and lowered his balls over my mouth.

"Lick them."

Oh dear God, yes. Yes. Yes. Yes.

I reached my tongue out and swiped his balls. He lowered himself farther, so they were pressed against my lips, and I bathed them with my tongue. When the pressure on my mouth increased, I understood what he wanted and I opened my mouth to suck first one and then the other testicle.

My nose was pressed into his groin and I was filled with his musky scent. That and the taste and feel of his balls in my mouth were incredible aphrodisiacs. I fought for control of my testicles, hoping I could keep them from spewing my passion all over my stomach. That task was made even more difficult when Clark removed one of his hands from my wrist and I could feel motion above me as Clark started stroking himself.

Watching a guy jerk off was erotic in any circumstance. Watching my lover do it was even more so. But watching him do it while he had my body pinned down and was forcing me to lick and suck his balls, well, that made my cock harder than it had ever been, and my balls ache.

I wiggled my hips, unable to stop them from moving. The smell of Clark's body, the taste of his sweat and musk in my mouth, the feel of his heat and strength overpowering me, they were so damn arousing I didn't think I'd be able to stave off an orgasm.

I thought of sad stories, counted backward, replayed baseball games in my mind, but none of those things worked. Just as the tingle started and I thought I wouldn't be able to stop my body from spilling its seed, I found the one thing that could hold me back—my desire to obey Clark. Somehow that stopped me from coming while simultaneously making me even harder.

Clark rose up and pulled his balls from my mouth with a popping sound. Then he pointed his cock toward my mouth. I licked my lips and opened as wide as I could while he slowly lowered himself into me. It had been a long time since I'd taken Clark's dick in my mouth, or any dick for that matter, because I hadn't been with other guys while he was gone. And he was huge. I mean, seriously hung. But I had spent a lot of intimate time with toys in both ends of my body over the past three years, so the invasion wasn't more than I could handle.

Clark settled his dick all the way into my mouth and throat until I could feel his balls and pubes against my face. He leaned over my body and sucked my dick into his mouth as he pumped his into mine. I loved the feeling of the warm, silky skin covering his hardness. No dildo felt like that. I moaned and whimpered around his cock, turned on beyond belief at the knowledge that he was controlling both his pleasure and mine.

It took every ounce of self-restraint I had not to come, but I started feeling concerned that I'd lose that battle. It all felt so damn good. Then Clark gave a hard suck to my cock and pulled his mouth off it. I missed the feeling of his mouth on me, but I was relieved at the loss because I figured it would allow me to maintain control of my impending orgasm.

He pushed himself up and braced his hands on the mattress with his legs still straddling my face and his dick still fucking my mouth. I expected him to pump harder into me in that new position, but he didn't. Instead, he dropped his dick all the way into my mouth and down my throat so far I couldn't breathe. Then he held himself perfectly still above me, reached his hand over to my dick, and ran one finger up the length of my cock as he spoke quietly.

"Come, Noah. Now."

My hips thrust up and I exploded with the most powerful orgasm I'd ever had. Clark didn't move his dick until I was done shooting hot cum all over my stomach and chest, so I couldn't breathe through it, which, oddly enough, seemed to heighten the sensation. When he finally pulled his hard cock out of my mouth, I gasped for air.

"So good, Clark."

It was hard to get the words out, my throat ached and my lungs burned, but I needed him to know.

"That was so, so good."

He gently moved my body so I was no longer hanging off the bed, put a pillow under my head, and got on the bed next to me. He peppered me with kisses—my neck, the spot behind my ear, and my cheek.

"I love you, Noah."

I wanted to wrap my arms around him, but my body was completely boneless from that experience.

"Me too, Clark. Love you so much. That was wonderful, angel. Thank you."

He nuzzled my neck and pressed his warm body against mine. That was when his hardness brushed against my leg and I realized he hadn't come. I wrapped my hand around his hard cock.

"Hey. What's this? Why didn't you finish?"

He threw one leg over my body, holding himself above me by pressing his forearms on the mattress.

"I wanted to concentrate on you, make sure you were enjoying yourself and that we didn't take things too far."

He peered into my eyes.

"That was what you needed, right, Noah?"

There was a conversation at the end of that question. A conversation about our sex life and what turned me on. Hell, I'd been expecting to talk to him about it anyway, thinking I'd need to explain what I wanted. But based on that little session, I gathered he probably already had the idea and our talk would be more about confirmation. The conversation could wait until later. After we got some sleep, and sure as hell after he got off.

"Almost, angel. I need one more thing."

He leaned down and kissed me, and then he licked his way down my neck to my ear.

"Anything, Noah. Just tell me, I'll give you anything."

There was a certain amount of desperation in those words, but I couldn't focus on it right then. I needed him to come. So I pushed my hand in between us and wrapped it around his cock, and then I stroked him the way I remembered he enjoyed it. Not too tight a grip, long, slow strokes intermingled with quick ones. And I whispered into his ear the entire time, telling him how much I loved him and how good he'd made me feel. It didn't take long before my hand was covered in cum and Clark was moaning in my ear.

He got up to go into the bathroom and came back with a wet washcloth to wipe off my body. After that, I finally relaxed completely and drifted off to sleep. My last conscious sensation was reaching for Clark's balls while he whispered in my ear.

"Thank you for letting me come home, Noah. I love you."

CHAPTER FOURTEEN

Noah—Present

WHEN I woke up, Clark and I were in the exact same position as when we fell asleep: his body tucked into mine, my hand cupping his balls, our arms around each other and legs tangled together, and his head buried in my neck. I kissed the top of his head and felt him smile in response.

"Were you already awake or was that just a sleeping-beauty moment?"

He kissed my neck, licked his way down my chest, and suckled my nipple. I moaned, buried my fingers in his hair, and pulled him up to my mouth for a long, messy kiss. Our mouths were locked together, tongues exploring, hands running wild over bare flesh when my stomach interrupted with a loud growl. Clark laughed.

"Hmmm. Trying to tell me something, sweetheart? Please, don't hold back. No reason for subtlety."

"Not trying to tell you anything. Damn stomach is a total cock-blocker. I'm thinking of having it permanently removed."

Clark gave a light bite to my earlobe and sat up.

"How about I feed you instead? Give me a minute to see whether there's anything edible in the kitchen. Otherwise, I'll go pick something up."

I wove my fingers with his.

"Don't want you to leave."

"Aw, sweetheart. I'm so sorry for hurting you like I did. I shouldn't have left, Noah. Please believe me when I tell you that it won't happen again. No matter what, I'll stand by you."

"I won't ever give you reason to leave again. I cherish you, Clark. I'll make sure you never doubt that."

I raised my body so I was sitting behind Clark and rested my head on his back.

"I'll come help in the kitchen."

"You're supposed to be taking it easy, Noah. You can come keep me company, but you sit and that's it."

We walked into the kitchen with our arms around each other. That wasn't new or a result of our separation. From day one, Clark had been an extremely affectionate boyfriend. He doted on me and always found reasons for our bodies to touch and connect. I loved that about him, loved how he made me feel, loved how proud he was of us as a couple.

I sat at the kitchen table, watched Clark go through the refrigerator and throw just about everything out, and felt grateful he was back. I'd been so alone, so incredibly incomplete without him.

"I'm not even opening some of these containers. You were in that hospital for six weeks. No chance these things are still edible."

When the fridge was empty, he dug through the freezer and found some bagels, sausages, and tater tots.

"Okay, this isn't going to be the breakfast of champions, but it'll curb that growling stomach of yours. I'll go grocery shopping later today when you're taking a nap."

"No way. I don't sleep alone ever again. We'll go to the store together. It's good for me to walk around. Think of it as physical therapy."

Clark must have liked my comment, because he dropped the food on the counter, walked over to me, and gave me a soft, sweet kiss.

"Love you, Noah."

AFTER BREAKFAST, we took a shower, hit the grocery store, and then settled on the couch in our sweats. I sat with my back against the sofa arm, and Clark sat between my legs, leaning against my chest. He had his laptop and typed away for a few hours while I flipped through channels and pretended to watch television. In reality, I was just enjoying the feeling of Clark's body, the knowledge that he was home with me, and the calmness and security he always brought to me.

"There's no way I can concentrate on work if you keep doing that."

"Doing what? I haven't moved."

He shifted his ass and I realized my hard-on had grown to the point where it was pressing insistently against its favorite location.

"Mmmm. I love feeling you up against me, Noah."

Clark kept rubbing and I thought I'd lose my mind if he didn't let me in.

"Jesus, Clark. It's been three years. Are you going to make me beg?"

He snickered and kept up the light touch without giving me anything more. Then he set the laptop on the floor, stripped off his clothes, and leaned over my prone body.

"You want my ass, Noah?"

I nodded and licked my lips, hoping I wasn't drooling.

"Okay. But we do this my way. Sit up."

I scrambled into a sitting position, my heart racing, my cock trying to poke a hole in my pants. Clark pulled my sweats down over my erection, and let the elastic snap against my balls.

"Ungh! Fuck."

He was leaning over me, looking into my eyes.

"Feel good?"

I threw my head back against the couch and stared at him.

"Yeah." I swallowed. "Yes, that feels good."

Clark nodded in understanding.

"Then we'll keep it there. Let you feel the pressure on your balls while I'm fucking myself on your prick. Still keep the lube in the nightstand drawer?"

"Uh-huh."

I gasped the words out as my body trembled with anticipation and arousal. Clark stood back up and walked to the bedroom. When he returned with the half-empty bottle of lube, he had a smirk on his face.

"Looks like you've been a busy boy while I was gone, Noah."

I had a moment of panic, not wanting him to think there had been other men in our bed.

"I didn't use it with anyone else. It was just when I was alone, getting myself off. There was nobody else. I promise."

Clark's eyes softened and he closed the distance between us immediately; his hand stroked my cheek and he kissed me gently.

"Shhh. I know that, sweetheart. I was just teasing because I saw all your new toys. That drawer is pretty full. I can't wait to try them on you."

I nodded and blinked back tears. Damn it. How long would it take me to forget what I'd done and put that chapter of our lives behind us? He said he forgave me and I knew he meant it. So I had to find a way to forgive myself, or else the past would keep shadowing our future.

All thoughts flew out of my head when I saw Clark wetting his fingers and reaching behind his back. I couldn't see him penetrate his ass, but the look on his face and his legs shifting farther apart told me exactly what he was doing. My dick was drooling and my balls were aching from a need for release and the pressure of the elastic digging into them. Fuck, that felt good. When Clark finished prepping himself, he covered my dick with Wet, pulled me to the edge of the sofa, then turned his back to me and straddled my legs.

"You don't move, Noah. I'm in charge."

I dug my fingers into the couch cushions, planted my feet on the ground, and watched my lover lower himself over my cock. He had pulled it off my stomach and was holding it out with one of his hands while he braced himself with his other hand. He found his pucker and pushed down against my dick until I broke through the tight ring of muscle and slipped into surging heat.

Clark slid his ass down my shaft and I could feel his channel stretching to accommodate me. When he finally took me in completely, his ass settled on my balls and my cock filling him, we both groaned. I wanted to thrust up and move my dick in and out of that tight heat, but he had told me not to move.

"Please." I finally let out a plea. "Please help me come."

Clark moaned and rolled his hips, then raised and lowered himself on my dick. He tugged me in deep, then moved up until just my crown remained imbedded in his body.

"Feels good, Clark. So good."

"Touch me, Noah. Stroke my cock while I fuck myself on yours."

"Jesus, yes."

I moved my hand from the death grip I had on the couch and enjoyed the smooth warmth of Clark's cock. His hips snapped and I knew he had hit his spot with my cock when he gasped. Then he increased his speed and kept the same angle as he raised and lowered himself on my dick in rapid succession. My hand flew on his dick in a desperate attempt to bring him off.

"Clark, I'm right there, right fucking there. Please let me. Jesus, fuck. Please."

Just when I thought I'd cry with denied need, Clark threw his head back against my shoulder and shouted.

"Now, Noah. Come with me now."

I bit his neck and filled him deep with my seed as I felt wet heat slide over my fingers. I moved my hand to my mouth and licked his cum off it while he looked back over his shoulder and watched me. Clark's blue eyes darkened and he reached his tongue out and joined my lips and fingers.

"So fucking hot, Noah. You drive me crazy."

Clark—Past

I STOOD aside so he'd have room to walk into the apartment, but neither of us said a word. We just gazed at each other. I shut the door behind him, never taking my eyes off his. Then I closed the distance between us slowly. I figured he could stop me if he didn't want me to get closer, but he didn't. Instead, he whimpered, dropped his bag, and closed his eyes when my lips met his.

The memory of my first kiss with Noah, my first kiss with anyone, my *only* kiss with anyone, had gotten me through many lonely nights. Over the years, I thought I'd blown it up in my mind, that it couldn't possibly have been as incredible as I'd remembered. But that second kiss told me that, if anything, I'd forgotten the details and how good it'd actually been.

Soft lips, warm breath on my face, his tongue playing with mine, his arms wrapped around me, holding me close, his muscular chest pressed against mine, my arms around his neck and my fingers playing with his hair. And a feeling I definitely hadn't experienced when we were leaning over the car console kissing—his hardness pressing against mine. My cock had filled so quickly that my knees almost buckled. I was certain I could come in my pants just from that—kissing Noah and feeling his aroused body against me. But I wanted more.

I moved my hand down his chest, over his nipples,

rubbed his stomach, and pushed my way under his shirt.

"Ungh."

Noah moaned when our skin made contact. It had to be the hottest damn sound I'd ever heard. I pushed my hand down over his hard dick and we both trembled.

Okay, if the fact that I still hadn't developed any interest in girls and the many hours I'd spent over the past four years watching man-on-man porn weren't enough to convince me, the fact that I was becoming completely undone by the feeling, smell, and taste of Noah, were most certainly enough to seal the deal: I was gay. *Well, Mom*, I thought to myself, *I guess we know where things went. Thank fucking goodness.*

"Tell me what you want, Noah," I mumbled into his neck as I gnawed on his skin.

He pulled away reluctantly and bent down by his duffel bag. Then he opened a side pocket with shaky hands and fumbled through it.

"Tell me what we can do. I brought my birth certificate to prove I'm eighteen, my admissions paperwork to prove I'm enrolled in State, so we're in the same stage of life, or whatever, and test results showing I'm clean for every fucking disease known to man. They're in here, let me find them."

"I know when your birthday was, and I trust you on the rest of it, Noah."

I bent over to pull him up to his feet and the back of

his neck came into my line of sight. I ran my fingers down the row of numbers running from the bottom of his hairline, down his long neck, to his shirt collar.

"What is this? Did you get a tattoo? "

He covered my hand with his, gave me a squeeze, then spoke in a gravelly voice.

"It's a constant reminder of the day I knew there was a reason to keep going, a reason to be a decent man. The day I met my angel."

032396...

March 23, 1996, the date I met Noah. He had branded himself for me. I groaned with arousal, ran my tongue over the numbers imprinted in his skin, turned him around, and sucked up a mark on the front of his neck. I was suddenly filled with an overwhelming desire to keep going until his entire body was covered with evidence that I owned him.

"Do you like it, Clark?"

"Oh hell yeah. Makes me feel like you belong to me."

"That's because I do belong to you. Always have. Always will, angel."

I groaned, dug my fingers into his firm ass, and pulled his crotch against mine.

"Do you want to go to the bedroom?"

Noah clutched me tightly, panting. Eventually, he seemed to get his breathing under control. He let go of my body and picked his duffel bag back up.

"Fuck, yes. If I don't get some action soon, my dick is

going to buy a one-way ticket to someone else's pants."

He walked toward the hallway leading to the bedroom. Oh, what a great ass. I made a low, throaty moan, swallowed hard, and followed my future.

CHAPTER FIFTEEN

Noah—Present

WE SAT on the couch together, reveling in the afterglow. I wrapped my arms around Clark and held him tight, feeling settled and calm deep down.

"Mmm. I like it when you take control."

He sighed and kissed the side of my neck.

"I know. Sorry I didn't do enough of that before. I was young and I didn't understand."

I nuzzled his neck.

"I don't want you to do anything you don't feel comfortable doing, angel. It has to work for both of us or it won't work at all, you know?"

He stood up and my cock slipped out of his ass, making us both groan. Then he pulled on his pants and shirt, raised my sweats back up, sat down next to me, and looked into my eyes.

"Noah?"

"Yeah?"

"Can we stop with the pronouns now and call a spade

a spade?"

I nodded.

"Domination, I can handle. But I can't hurt you, sweetheart. Not really. I mean some light bondage, maybe a little spanking is fine, but full on torture or humiliation I just can't do. And I can't do it in public. None of it. It has to stay between us, just like the rest of our lovemaking."

It pleased me to no end that Clark not only understood my needs, but saw them as an extension of our love and not as some depraved, twisted sickness.

"You've given this a lot of thought, haven't you?"

"Of course I have. I've spent a lot of time wondering if one of the reasons you cheated is that you weren't satisfied with our sex life, that I didn't give you what you wanted in and out of the bedroom. I want to please you, Noah. I want that so much. But I don't know how far I can take things."

I closed my eyes and tried to explain what I wanted.

"I just..."

Clark stroked my arms, then took my hands in his and squeezed them as I tried to find my words.

"You know how when we go out to eat, you order for me?"

He nodded.

"I like that. With you, I mean. Not with anyone else. With the rest of the world, I feel like I have to be on guard all the time, like they might want something, do something, or say something. I can't show weakness. I have to be strong.

I have to be in complete control. But when I'm with you, I can shut down all my defenses and let go. It's not just that I *can* give over control to you; it's that I love doing it. It makes me feel safe and cared for. I don't want you to humiliate me, I don't want us to take our sex life on the road, and I'm not interested in serious pain. When I submit to you, when you're in charge, it feels like I have no worries in the world, because you're handling things, you're taking care of me. That's what I want. Does that make any sense?"

Clark kissed me deeply and I saw tears in his eyes.

"Yeah, it does. It's also sexy as hell. I love taking care of you, sweetheart. In and out of bed."

I dropped my forehead against his and felt the tension release from my body. I couldn't even be amazed at how easy that conversation had been, because that was how things always were between us. We had always been on the same page.

Clark—Past

WHEN WE got to the bedroom, Noah dropped his duffel bag and turned to look at me. We were standing about a foot and a half apart from each other at the end of the bed. I kept expecting awkwardness to seep into the air. We hadn't seen each other in four years, after all. Yes, we'd talked on the phone religiously, but that wasn't the same thing. Plus, other than that goodbye kiss, we'd never had a physical relationship. Anyway, there was no awkwardness. Instead, the air was filled with heat and anticipation.

Noah reached down and pulled off his henley and the T-shirt underneath it in one movement. I admired his defined chest while he toed off his shoes, then removed his belt, opened the button on his pants, and pushed them down to the ground. Without realizing what I was doing, I had been removing my clothes in step with him, so by the time he was standing naked in front me, I was naked in front of him. We drank each other in, gazes roaming over each other's bodies.

Why he'd want to look at me when he could just stare in a mirror was beyond me. The man was stunning. His chest and shoulders were broad and muscular. His skin was tan all over and covered with a light sprinkling of dark hair that culminated in enticing curls at the base of his hard cock. And those hazel eyes captivated me, just as they had the first night I'd met him.

"You're so beautiful, Clark. You've always been so very beautiful."

I blushed and shook my head. He was striking, stunning. I trembled with a need to touch that magnificent body.

"Can I... I want to... Will you let me taste you, Clark?"

Oh, now, that was about the sexiest thing ever. Strong,

tough Noah Forman standing in front of me completely naked and asking for permission to suck me off.

I sat down at the end of the bed and spread my knees in invitation. He walked over and dropped to his knees between mine. Then he bent his head forward and licked my balls. Oh Jesus. That felt so fucking good!

His hands were on my hips, holding me tight, and he was mouthing, licking, and sucking on my balls with serious gusto. I could hear the slurping intermingled with his moans. Every once in a while, he'd move his face up from my balls and run his cheek over my cock. His stubble grazed against the sensitive skin of my cockhead and I lost it.

"Oh. Oh. Oh. Noah, that's so good. So damn good. I'm gonna. Gonna. Oh!"

When he heard those words, Noah raised his head and took my crown into his mouth. Then he sucked on it as I spilled my seed into him. I heard his muffled groans as I shot and felt wet warmth on my leg.

"Jesus, Noah!"

I gasped and then reached down so I could put my hands under his arms and pull him up. He stood between my knees and I found myself face-to-face with his still hard cock, dripping with cum.

"Did you get off just from sucking me?"

I licked the cum off his dick, taking more time than was absolutely necessary to get the job done. I'd spent so many lonely nights fantasizing about Noah—what the grown-up version would look like naked and hard, how his skin would taste, how his dick would feel against my tongue. As I tasted his cum on my tongue, I decided that the answer to all three questions was the same: hot, arousing, and addictive.

"I'm sorry. I just…you're just… I couldn't help it."

I rose to my feet. We were standing, pressed together, and I looked into his eyes.

"Don't apologize. That's the sexiest thing I can imagine. I love knowing that I turn you on so much, sweetheart."

I tensed when the endearment left my mouth. Where had that come from?

"Oh man."

Noah panted the words out and then our lips met again. I mouthed his bottom lip between mine, then his top lip, and finally his tongue. We pressed our tongues into each other's mouths and sucked and moaned together. Then we both crawled onto the bed and shoved the covers away until we could get underneath them.

Noah rolled on top of me, connecting our bodies from head to toe. He was warm and hard and perfect. I flipped him onto his back and kissed him deeply.

"Mph! Clark, please."

He thrust his dick up. I growled and sucked another mark up on his neck as I moved my hands all over his body, tweaking nipples, feeling the hair on his stomach leading down to his dick, squeezing his balls. And all the while, I kept sucking and licking his neck and his chest.

"Oh, Clark! I need you to fuck me. Please, oh, please. *Fuck me!*"

I growled and bit his chest, sucked his nipples until they were hard pebbles standing at attention, and moved my hand from his balls and down his cleft.

"Yes!"

Noah pushed his ass down against my fingers. Damn, was he ever needy. What a giant fucking turn-on that was.

"I have to get something, Noah. I'm not sure what I have. Hold on. Let me check the medicine cabinet."

"I have a bottle of lube in the side pocket of my duffel bag."

He blushed and closed his eyes.

"Have you been planning this, sweetheart?"

"I've been planning this for about five years, Clark. And I *love* hearing you call me that."

I moved my hands to his face and stroked his cheeks.

"It's how I think of you. How I've thought of you for a long time, Noah. That okay?"

He kissed me tenderly.

"Better than."

I rubbed my nose against his, nuzzled his neck, then scrambled off the bed to find the lube. The bottle was right where he said it'd be. I noticed it hadn't been opened and smiled to myself. Then I crawled up the bed and kneeled between Noah's legs.

I poured some lube onto my fingers and moved them

up and down his cleft before concentrating on the tight ring of muscles at his opening. I massaged that area gently until he relaxed, then I pushed a finger in.

"Ahh."

Noah moaned, but didn't pull away. I curled my finger up and moved it around until I felt the smooth ball inside, and massaged it as I took Noah's dick into my mouth and sucked on it.

I couldn't get all of him down my throat, like I'd seen the guys do in porn, but I figured maybe I just needed more practice. Noah didn't seem to mind, anyway. He was moaning and whimpering, calling my name, and clutching my head as I continued to lick and suck him into my mouth while I added a second and then a third finger into his ass and scissored them apart so I could stretch him and get him ready for me.

I'm not like Mister Hung or anything. Well, I didn't think I was, anyway. It's not like I had a clue how big other guys were when they got hard. But I knew I was as big as a few of those porn actors, and at least a couple of inches bigger than Noah, and I didn't want to hurt him.

I was concentrating on Noah, enjoying his moans, the warmth of his body surrounding my fingers, the feeling and taste of his cock on my tongue, when he pulled my head off him.

"I'm on the edge, Clark. And I want to finish with you inside me."

I kissed the tip of his cock, poured more lube onto

my fingers, and pushed it inside him. Then I sat back on my haunches and draped Noah's thighs over mine. I bent down over him, lined my cock up with his opening, and pushed in past the ring of muscles.

Noah made a noise that sounded like a whimper, so I stopped and kissed him.

"Do you want me to pull it out? Is it too much?"

He grasped my hips and held me in place.

"Don't you dare! You just have a huge dick. But, it feels good—different, but good. Don't stop."

So I didn't. I pushed in slowly as I kissed his cheeks, sucked on his earlobe, and licked his neck. It didn't take long for me to feel his pubes against me and I knew I was all the way in.

"You feel so good inside, Noah. So hot and tight. Is this okay? Can I move?"

His eyes were closed and he was panting.

"Feels good for me too. Yes, move. Fuck me."

Thank goodness I had just come because, otherwise, I'd have lost it right then. I was pretty damn close to blowing again as it was. I moved myself in and out of Noah, enjoying the feeling of his body inside and out. We moaned together and he scratched his nails up and down my back while I licked and sucked the beads of sweat off his neck.

I changed the angle of my thrusts until I hit the right spot and Noah's entire body shook.

"There! Right there."

I kept pressing my cock against that spot over and over again. Our bodies were sweaty and Noah's dick was trapped between our stomachs, rubbing on our wet skin while I moved in and out of him.

"Oh, make me come...please, Clark...harder...oh! There...harder...gonna...so close... Please make me come... yes!"

Wetness spread between our stomachs as his dick pulsed and his ass tightened around my cock, and then I lost it. I held his shoulders tight and pushed my dick in as far as I could, unloading deep into his bowels while letting out a triumphant shout.

"Oh God. Oh God. Oh God. That felt so good. You're so good at that, Clark."

I kissed him and held him close to me. Eventually, I lifted my head up, brushed his hair off his face, and looked into his eyes. He looked dazed and satisfied, but also a little sad.

"What's wrong, Noah?"

He blushed and turned away, but he didn't lie. Noah never lied to me.

"I'm being a jackass. Don't worry about it."

"What are you talking about? Tell me."

"I'm just feeling a little jealous. I didn't realize you'd been with other guys. I mean, of course you have. You've been in college alone for four years. I'm being stupid."

I kissed him and licked his lips.

"I haven't been with anyone else, ever. You're my first, Noah. First everything."

He looked surprised and happy.

"Yeah?"

I nodded.

"Mmm-hmm. If you didn't know that, you shouldn't have let me do this without a condom. Please don't ever let anyone do that, sweetheart."

"You're not just anyone. I trust you. I know you'd never hurt me. Hell, you wouldn't touch me no matter how much I threw myself at you. And besides, there'll never be anyone else now that I have you."

I loved hearing that, wanted it to be true more than anything, but I didn't want to cage Noah in. He was still so young.

"Noah, you don't have to make me that promise. I know you've been with other guys, but you're just eighteen and you might want more experiences. Besides, I'm kind of a boring person. Not like your other friends."

He put his hands on my cheeks and held my face right in front of his.

"Clark?"

"Yeah?"

"I was willing to put up with the whole 'you're only thirteen so you must not really know what you're feeling' shit when I was a kid. It was bullshit and I knew it, but I was willing to put up with it. That's done now. I'm an adult and I know what I want. I've wanted to be with you since that first day I saw you in my bedroom. Like an angel come to rescue me. *My* angel. Getting to know you just increased that want. I would rather do nothing with you every day of the week than everything with anyone else. And after what we just did, man, you are not going to be able to shake me. *Ever.*"

I thought about insisting he think about it, telling him that he had a long life ahead of him and I'd wait. But I'd been waiting for him for so long already. And hadn't I been his age when I went to school? I hadn't met any other guys, never had any interest in other guys. So how was that any different? Noah was right; he was an adult and I had to trust him to know his feelings.

"Okay. Thank you, sweetheart."

He smiled, cuddled up against me as tight as possible, buried his head in my neck, and cupped my balls in his big hand.

"Oh, and Clark?"

"Yeah?"

"There haven't been other guys. Well, there were before we met and a few more after that. But they were just hand jobs and blow jobs. Nothing else. I stopped messing around with other guys completely after that couple of days I spent at Pat's house when I was all tweaked out. So, you're my first too."

"Really? But you said..."

"Really. And I didn't say anything different. You

assumed and I didn't correct you, because I wanted you and I thought that would improve my odds. Make you feel less like you were taking advantage of me or something. Not that it worked. Who knows, maybe I would have fucked the whole gay population of Emile City if you hadn't come around. But you did and I didn't. So here we are, a couple of ex-virgins with a new bottle of lube and an entire summer ahead of us before classes start. Any ideas of what we can do to pass the time?"

CHAPTER SIXTEEN

Noah—Present

I WOKE up alone. Again. Three years of waking up alone and I still wasn't used to it, still hated it. But it was different this time. This time, I could smell him on the sheets. I pressed myself into the pillow next to me. Yup, that was Clark, not just an elaborate version of my usual dreams—dreams of Clark laughing, Clark moaning, Clark coming, Clark…just Clark.

I rubbed the sleep from my eyes and it all came back to me—the fact that Clark had come back to me. The heaviness lifted from my heart and the stomach pain that had been my constant companion for the past three years cleared away. The sheets felt cold, so he must have been up for longer than a middle-of-the-night trip to the can.

I shuffled out of bed and found him in the living room, sitting on the couch. He was curled into a ball, trying to keep warm. I walked back to the bedroom, dragged the blanket off the bed, and took it to the couch.

"Hey. You okay?"

He looked up at me and smiled.

"Yeah. Just couldn't sleep. Didn't want to wake you by tossing and turning in bed, so I came out here."

I sat next to him and wrapped the blanket around us. Clark put his head on my shoulder and drew figure eights on my chest with his finger.

"If you'd have woken me, you could've *tossed* my salad, *turned* me over, and fucked me until you *came* in our bed. That surely would have helped you sleep."

I hoped I wasn't being too explicit, but after the previous night, I figured we were done skirting around my sexual needs, and I could make jokes without upsetting him.

"Wow, Noah. That's impressive even for you. You turned that sentence into a double entendre in three ways with one move."

I chuckled and waggled my eyebrows.

"What can I say? You inspire me. I'll show you how much in a minute, but first talk to me about what's been keeping you up all night."

He didn't say anything for a long couple of minutes.

"We've already established that the bed is the same. And this is our old couch and coffee table. I recognize the dining room table too. The only thing missing is…"

"I burned it."

He coughed out a surprised response.

"What?"

"My grandma's plaid armchair. The one I was sitting in that night. I torched the fucker. Covered it with a bottle of kerosene and lit a match."

He pulled his head off my chest and stared at me.

"Jesus, Noah!"

"I made sure it was in the middle of a big concrete pad, no combustibles around. Still, that polyester fabric burned like a motherfucker. Singed my eyebrows. Totally worth it."

He lowered his eyes and his voice.

"Why did you do it?"

"Because looking at it reminded me of the moment in time when I fucked up both of our lives. It was either burn the chair or..."

"That's not what I meant."

His voice was a whisper. I had to take a second to process what he'd said, and then I understood. But before I could answer, he spoke again.

"I spent so much time being angry, Noah. At first, I was angry with you. Angry that you were cheating, angry that you were doing it in our home, angry that you were doing it where you had to know I was likely to see. After that, I was angry with myself. Angry that I missed the signs, angry that I wasn't giving you what you needed to the point where you wanted someone else, and angry that I drove you to a place where you wanted me to see you doing it. You had to know I'd walk in on you. You set me up, right?"

My voice raced out.

"Yes, Clark, but it's not like—"

"Yeah. You set me up. So that sucked, when I realized

it. I was happy and I thought you were too. I hated that I was so out of touch with you, with what you needed. It made me question everything, made feel like I could never really please you.

"For years I played the scene from that night over and over in my mind. I wondered how many guys there had been before that one. I wondered how many hints I had missed before you felt like you had to bring him into our home and set me up to catch you. I thought that if only I hadn't been so dense, I would have realized that you were dissatisfied with our life and then maybe I could have changed and been what you wanted or maybe you just needed a break, you were so young when we got together, maybe you just wanted more experiences, or maybe…"

I could think of only one way to get him to stop talking, so I could get control over the conversation. I climbed onto his lap, straddled him, and pillaged his mouth with mine. Filling him up with my tongue finally made the words stop and the moans start. The taste of him in my mouth and the feel of his body against mine almost distracted me, but explaining the reason for my stupidity three years prior was too important to ignore. I pulled my mouth off his and smiled at his dazed expression.

"My turn." I nuzzled his neck. "I have to explain what happened that night, because you need to understand that there weren't any other guys and that I was happy, angel. I was so damn happy and satisfied with you and our life."

He looked confused.

"Then why, Noah? Why did you push me away like that?"

"Because I wanted to prove that you wouldn't leave me. I wanted to prove that you'd stay with me no matter what."

Nothing from Clark. Just a shocked expression and his mouth hanging open in disbelief.

"Yeah. I know. Not my finest hour. I had it all planned out. You'd walk in on us, I'd apologize, you'd forgive me, and then he'd understand. But when I saw the hurt in your eyes, I realized how stupid I was being. Realized I didn't need to prove anything to him. Realized there were some things that can't be forgiven, like how much I clearly hurt you in that moment."

Clark was shaking his head, eyes closed, brow furrowed.

"I don't under...so many questions...who is *he*? Who didn't you need to prove anything to?"

"Ben."

"Your brother? What does your brother have to do with this?"

I thought about lying or deflecting or refusing to answer him. How many more times could my brother hurt Clark? But I owed him the truth.

"We fought that day. After he called and I met him. We fought about all the usual things—me being gay, my family being homophobic. You know the drill. Ben was mad I hadn't come home for Christmas. I said I wasn't going to go to a place where we weren't welcome. He said it wasn't fair of me to expect my family to understand my *lifestyle choice.*"

I snickered at that last bullshit gem and rolled my eyes, then continued.

"I said my family should support me and want to be with me no matter what; that their love should be unconditional. He said nothing was unconditional, including your feelings for me. I told him he was wrong. He challenged me to prove it. I clearly lost my fucking mind, because I agreed. That's when he threw down the gauntlet. He said if I expected my family to support me no matter who I wanted to sleep with, then I should expect the same of you."

Clark was still stunned, but he also looked sad and horrified. Tears filled his eyes and spilled down his face. I thought he'd say sibling fighting was the stupidest reason in the world to do what I'd done, but he didn't. Instead, he trembled and his voice shook as he responded to my explanation of why I'd ruined our lives.

"And I proved him, right. I did exactly what he said I'd do—I left you. I'm so sorry, Noah."

Damn it all to fucking hell. No! I wasn't going to let him feel bad about this.

"Clark, stop it. First off, you're here, aren't you? So that means he was wrong. And, to be clear, I *always* knew you'd be back. Besides, there's a huge difference between expecting my parents to accept who I want to sleep with—something that has absolutely nothing to do with them—and expecting my lover to accept me sleeping around on him. Especially without talking about it first. Even more so in our home. And to shove it in your face like that.

"It was too much, way too much. But I didn't realize it until you were standing in front of me with pain in your eyes. And by then it was too late, the damage was done. So I froze, no words came out, and then you were gone."

Tears ran down his face and he wiped them away with the back of his hand.

"I didn't leave because you cheated. I could have gotten past it. It wouldn't have been easy, it hurt like hell, but I could have. I stopped being mad about the blow job long before I left the city limits."

He swallowed, composed himself, and continued.

"What I couldn't get over was you sitting there and not saying a word. Every time I picked up the phone to call you, every time I got in the car to drive home, every time I wanted to mail a letter I'd written, every damn time I did any of those things, I'd remember you looking at me and not saying anything. I'd remember that you wanted me to catch you with him. And I knew you wanted me to leave. You wanted us to be over and you just couldn't end it yourself, so you pushed me to do it for you."

"Oh, Clark. No…"

"So that's been my justification all these years. That I

was doing what you wanted me to do. That I was being strong and proving how much I love you by staying away, like you wanted. But I was stupid. I should have talked to you, asked you why, and then tried to fix it. It took me three years to figure that out, but as soon as I did, I came back."

Well, there was nothing else to say at that point. Yeah, I wished he hadn't left, but I understood. Hell, I'd understood when I thought he'd left because I cheated one time. Leaving because he'd thought I'd been doing it for a while and I'd orchestrated having him catch me because I'd wanted him gone was an even better reason. Besides, he was back, just as I'd always known he would be.

"Well, let's be grateful that nightmare interlude in our lives is over and we've moved on. You're back now and everything is okay."

The chords in his neck were pulsing and his body was tense.

"Just like that? I walk back in and the last three years disappear? We're back together, back in sync, tight as always, like it was all just a bad nightmare. How is that possible? How can it be that easy, Noah?"

"Easy? You're saying being apart was easy for you? Because I felt like I was crawling out of my skin every day. I forced myself to eat and drink and sleep and breathe by sheer power of will, so I'd be whole once you came back to me."

"No, sweetheart. The being apart was pure misery. But us, coming back together, that's been easy and smooth since the day I walked into the hospital."

"Of course it has. We're right together, Clark. It's supposed to be easy and smooth. It shouldn't be hard when it's right. And it never has been hard for us, has it? Being together has always been the most natural thing in the world. It's the being apart that was wrong, so let's not do that again, 'kay?"

Clark's body finally relaxed. He kissed my cheek.

"As much as I wish I could, there's no way for me to go back to that night and handle things differently, Noah. I can't start over and give us back those years we lost. But I can promise you that, starting right now, we'll never be apart again. Not for any length of time. No matter what. I can promise you a happy ending."

I licked a line from the bottom of Clark's neck, up his chin, and over his lips.

"Can I have that happy ending right now?"

Clark moaned into my mouth and swiped his tongue in, plundering and tasting.

"Mmm-hmm."

We stumbled to the bedroom together, touching, rubbing, and kissing the entire time. When we got to the bed, I scrambled backward toward the headboard and looked up at Clark expectantly. My heart was racing, lungs working overtime to get air into my hyper-excited body. Clark crawled toward me with a gleam in his eye. Instinctively, I reached down and stroked my cock, watching him devour me with his heated gaze. When he got to my dick, he gave it a few swipes with his tongue, then he pushed my legs up and buried his face in my ass.

"Clark!"

He licked my cleft, poked at the ring of my muscles with his tongue, then alternately penetrated me and sucked on my pucker. I let go of my cock and took hold of my legs, underneath my knees, pulling them up and out. That gave Clark full use of his hands, which he promptly moved toward my asshole.

Seconds later, he had both of his thumbs and his tongue buried in me, feeling the walls of my cavity, pressing against that spot inside, and generally driving me out of my mind. My eyes rolled back in my head and noises left my body that sounded more animal than human. Somewhere in all of that, Clark must have removed his mouth from my ass, because I suddenly felt his thick, long cock enter me.

"Yes, Clark! Yes! Deep. Fuck me so deep."

He entangled his fingers with mine as he pummeled my hole, so damn hard, so damn deep, and so damn good. Our moans filled the air, both of us covered in a light sheen of sweat, our tongues occasionally meeting.

I tried to move my hand toward my cock so I could get that last bit of sensation and finish, but our interwoven hands prevented my movement.

"Gonna fuck the cum out of you, Noah."

Oh God. Oh God. Oh God. Between his monster dick

ripping into me, my body being pinned beneath his, hands restrained, and now those words, I was going to pass out from the pleasure.

"Feel me in you, Noah? So deep inside you? Gonna come so deep you'll be able to taste me."

I whimpered and kissed him. My entire body trembled. He intermingled every few words with a punishing thrust.

"Ready for me to breed you, sweetheart?"

I nodded. My entire body shook with need.

"I want to hear you say it, Noah. I want to hear you beg."

I threw my head back and tears of joy streamed down my face.

"Please fuck me, Clark. Please make me come. I need you to make me come."

His mouth pressed over mine, his tongue penetrated me, and he gave a final, triumphant push into my ass. Then he stilled inside me, his dick pulsing, his eyes closed, and my name flowing from his lips over and over again. He'd never looked more beautiful. I joined him in ecstasy with the most powerful orgasm I'd ever had.

Clark collapsed on top of me, sucked my neck, and tried to regulate his breathing. I stroked his back and whispered my love and devotion to him. Eventually, he pulled out of my ass and helped me climb from the bed. I leaned on him in the shower and stood there in a daze while he cleaned me.

By the time we got back into bed, it was almost sunrise

and we were both exhausted. I wrapped myself around Clark and smiled when he burrowed into my body, fitting all our nooks and crannies together. We really were so *right* together in every way. I slept soundly, warm in the knowledge that we were going to be okay.

CHAPTER SEVENTEEN

Noah—Present

"CLARK, I'M going stir-crazy. Between all that time in the hospital and now being cooped up at home, I need to go out."

It was Saturday afternoon; I was checking e-mails on my computer and Clark was working on his. I was feeling much better. I was even back to exercising, and I planned to go back to work part-time on Monday.

"I got an e-mail from Tim. Looks like a bunch of guys are going out tonight. There's karaoke at the Swallows Nest. Want to join them, angel?"

Clark closed his laptop.

"I haven't seen Tim and Frank since I left. How are they?"

My chest felt tight with the memory of those lost years. I tried to shake it off.

"They're doing well. At least I think they're doing well. I haven't seen them much. I, um, I sort of stopped hanging out with everyone when you left. But they still e-mail me every so often and invite me out. Luckily, tonight is one of those invite nights."

Clark pulled me onto his lap for a hug.

"Why did you stop spending time with our friends, sweetheart?"

I didn't have a good answer. Mostly, I didn't feel like breathing when he was gone, let alone socializing. So I just hit the pause button on my life and waited for him to come home.

"I don't know. It was easier that way, I guess. That way I didn't have to keep explaining why you weren't in town for a visit."

"Why would they expect you to explain that? I'd think they'd stop mentioning my name entirely, at least around you."

Oh, right. I forgot to mention that part.

"I didn't tell anyone what happened. They all think you were temporarily out of town for work. I didn't tell them I was a complete bastard and you took a break from our relationship."

Clark kissed my neck and licked and sucked his way up to my ear.

"Thank you."

"You're not mad?"

He kissed me, soft lips touching, tongue seeking entry, then pushing into my mouth. I melted against him.

"Not mad. I'm grateful you kept me from having to explain how I could have been so stupid. I'll never forgive myself for leaving you, Noah."

"Oh, angel, you have to, because I'll never forgive myself for driving you away. We can't both walk around carrying that guilt."

He stroked my temples with his fingers and flicked his tongue over my earlobes.

"It'll get better. Time will pass, and those years apart will become a fuzzy memory."

That was true. It already felt like we'd never been apart. Like maybe it had all just been a nightmare.

AS SOON as we walked toward the door at the Swallows Nest, I regretted my recommendation that we leave the house. There were only three guys in the parking lot and every single one of them was checking Clark out. The situation was bound to get worse when we got inside.

I relaxed my fists and let blood flow to my white knuckles while I put my arm around my angel and pulled him tightly against me. I needed to get a grip. Clark smiled at me and rested his head on my shoulder as we walked inside, completely oblivious to his admirers, as usual.

Our friend, Tim, was the first person to see us when we walked in. He rushed up, reached for Clark, then remembered himself and dropped his hands. Good.

"Hey, Clark! I can't believe you're here. It's been, what?

Two, three years? How long are you going to be in town?"

Clark reached his free hand up and squeezed Tim's shoulder, which resulted in a panicked look from Tim. Damn, was I really that bad? Well, yeah, I guess I was.

"I moved back, Tim. You'll be seeing a lot more of me. And, from what I understand, a lot more of this guy too."

Clark laughed and hugged me.

"Noah tells me that he's been on a social sabbatical, but that's over now."

Tim grinned.

"Glad to hear it. We've all missed you guys. Come on, let's find Frank. He'll be thrilled to see you."

We followed Tim to the bar. The bartenders were all wearing painted-on jeans and tight white T-shirts with the bar's name on them, only the words "the" and "nest" were in tiny print, leaving just a large "swallows" written across their chests. The bar had a new owner and name since Clark had last been there, so he was seeing those shirts for the first time. He laughed out loud. One of the guys behind the bar saw him and smirked.

"It's not false advertising, cutie. I'm happy to prove it to you. I'm going on break in ten minutes."

I pulled Clark up against my waist and glared at the bartender.

"We'll take your word for it, *cutie*. He's off-limits."

I heard a giggle next to me and turned to see Clark's eyes twinkling and his head shaking just a little as he looked at me. When I caught his eye, he gave me a tender kiss.

"Love you."

My anger melted away. I kissed him back, keeping it light at first, then deepening it. It didn't take long for our surroundings to disappear in my mind. Clark was my only focus. I ran my hands up and down his arms, then snaked them behind his waist and kneaded his tight ass.

"Damn, man. If you aren't going to share, at least take it somewhere private so the rest of us don't eat our hearts out."

I smirked at the bartender and let Clark lead me to where our friends were standing. Tim had found Frank talking to two men I didn't recognize. One of them was scowling at the other, his hip tilted to the side with his hand on it.

"Gurrl, if you didn't have such a tight ass and your mama's credit card, you couldn't get away with that piss-poor attitude."

He looked up when we got closer and raked his eyes over Clark's body. I opened my mouth to tell him off when Tim intervened.

"Frank, look who the cat dragged in. Clark's finally home. Oh, and Terry, if you've got a death wish, the fastest way to fulfill it is to hit on Clark. I highly recommend against it."

Terry rolled his eyes, made a humph sound, and pulled his friend off the barstool.

"Let's go back to my place and watch porn. I'm clearly

not getting any action here tonight. Do you think it's because I didn't accessorize enough?"

His friend laughed, put his arm around him as they walked away, and responded, "Bitch, the only accessory that would've matched that ensemble is a wand."

Frank laughed at his friends, then greeted us.

"Noah! Clark! Hey, guys. I'm so glad you came. It's been way too long."

Like Tim, Frank instinctively reached for a hug, looked at me, and moved his hand in front of his body for a shake instead. Clark looked at me tenderly, then shook Frank's hand and smiled. Yeah, it'd been three years, but our friends still remembered I was a possessive asshole who didn't like anyone else touching Clark. And Clark still didn't seem to mind.

It was funny, but I hadn't ever thought much of that in the past. It was truly my natural reaction, and I'd been with Clark since I was eighteen, so I'd never realized that it was unusual. But over the past three years, when I wasn't holed up in our house, fixing it up, I'd occasionally met up with our friends. For the first time, I'd done that without Clark by my side. He had always consumed most of my attention, so without him there I noticed other people more than I ever had. One thing that jumped out right away was that other guys weren't bothered by seeing their partners hugging friends. Some of them even shared kisses. Well, it bothered me, plain and simple. Men needed to keep their mitts off Clark. He was *mine.*

Just as those thoughts made their way through my mind, a little guy ran up to us, hopped up against Clark and wrapped his arms and legs around him. He kissed Clark soundly on the cheek with a loud smack.

"Hey, good-looking! Didn't expect to see you here. You're looking hot as ever. Those pants are doing a damn fine job of accentuating your beast."

Tim and Frank looked absolutely terrified. I was in shock. Nobody but me had ever come close to touching or talking to Clark that way. I would have torn the guy off my lover and taught him some manners, but he was so much smaller than me that it didn't seem like a fair fight.

Clark laughed deeply.

"It's great to see you, Zach! It was a last minute thing. Noah wanted to get out of the house."

Zach slid down off Clark and raised his head all the way up to look at me. Big brown eyes took over his beautiful pixie face.

"Oh shit, of course. Noah, I recognize you from all those fucking pictures in Clark's bedroom. It's great to finally meet you. And thank you for dragging Clark's sorry ass out, I'm in desperate need of a partner on stage."

I was so busy trying to process this angelic-looking sprite with the vocabulary of a sailor that I didn't fully register his comment about being in my angel's bedroom. He looked over at Clark and sighed.

"Aaron refuses to go up there. I'm all set to sing a Sonny and Cher duet and he turned me down flat. Said he doesn't want to sing in public, even if it's Cher. Cher! I swear, Clark, if he hadn't fucked and sucked me into oblivion this afternoon, I'd start questioning whether the man is actually playing for our team."

A deep voice from behind me joined the conversation.

"Not this again. I thought we'd resolved that question a long time ago. In this very bar, if I'm not mistaken."

I turned my head to see a tall blond with kind eyes. He walked up to us, looked at Zach adoringly, wrapped his arms around the smaller man, and kissed the top of his head. Zach's entire face lit up as he raised his gaze up to the blond, twined their fingers together, and kissed the back of his hand. Another kiss to Zach's head, and the taller man looked at Clark.

"Hey, Clark. Sorry we haven't been by your place. Things have been crazy with the move."

The blond let go of Zach, hugged Clark, then turned to me and wrapped his arms around me and pulled me into a hug. He was only a couple of inches shorter than me, so he was able to reach up and talk into my ear.

"You must be Noah. We've heard so much about you. We can't wait to get to know you better."

He patted my back, then dropped his arms from my shoulders and pulled Zach's body in front of his again, hunching over his shoulders and rubbing his stomach.

Clark's eyes were sparkling and a smile covered his face. He was clearly glad to see these guys, so I didn't want to make a scene. Plus, I wasn't angry so much as surprised.

"Noah, this is my good friend, Zach Johnson and his partner, Aaron Paulson. I met Zach when I first moved to LA, and he was a lifesaver. Showed me around, introduced me to his friends, even helped me find my apartment. And now he lives in EC West."

Aaron beamed down at his partner, but Zach just brushed off the compliments.

"Please, it was nothing. But if you think I was such a big fucking help, I'm calling in the damn favor. You're Sonny, I'm Cher, and we're up, so shake a dick and let's go."

Clark snorted out a laugh.

"I think the saying's shake a *leg*, Zach."

Zach kissed his partner, then took Clark's hand in his and pulled him away from me and toward the stage.

"Oh, please, Clark. Why in the hell would anyone want to shake a leg? Now, shaking dicks..."

Frank and Tim had been frozen in their spots, watching the entire exchange without saying a word. I was looking after Clark, trying to process what had just happened when I heard Tim's voice.

"Hey, Aaron, umm, you might want to tell Zach to take it easy with the touchy-feely stuff. Noah doesn't really, ummm..."

Aaron wrapped his arm around my shoulder and led

me toward a table in front of the stage, while he spoke to Tim and Frank over his shoulder.

"Don't worry about it, Tim. Zach and Clark are old friends. Besides, Noah doesn't have anything to worry about and he knows it."

He turned to me.

"You look great, Noah. Really great. When Clark told us you'd been in an accident, we were worried. But I can't tell that you're hurt at all."

I couldn't figure out why I wasn't more upset that Clark had been talking to Aaron or that, at that very moment, he was on stage with Zach, who was practically grinding into him while doing a damn good rendition of "I Got You, Babe." When we sat down and I saw the look of longing on Aaron's face as he watched Zach sing and the adoring look that Zach returned to him from the stage, I figured it out. Those two guys were completely gone over each other; neither of them was a threat. Good thing too, because Clark seemed to like them and so did I. I relaxed, drank my beer, and enjoyed being out with friends for the first time in way too long.

CHAPTER EIGHTEEN

Noah—Present

AFTER WE got home from the bar, Clark and I took a fast shower and got into bed. We lay on our sides, facing each other for a couple of seconds before Clark wrapped his arm around my waist and hauled me in so I was pressed against him from toe to dick to chest. I could feel his hard shaft and I knew he could feel mine. I didn't resist, just let him pull me close and place my body where he wanted.

"Did you have fun tonight?"

He moved his face toward mine and I tipped my head back in anticipation.

"Mmm-hmm. It was nice to get out, see all those guys again. And I really liked meeting your friends."

Clark licked the seam of my lips, and pushed inside when I opened to him. We kissed and touched, enjoying the comfort of being together.

"Zach's a great guy. He hasn't had it easy. So much so that I wondered whether he was even capable of having a relationship or any deep connection with another person.

He had always seemed so fun and happy on the outside, but locked-down and detached on the inside. When I met Aaron and saw the two of them together, I realized my concern was misplaced."

I sucked on Clark's neck, ran my hand down his chest over his dick and down to his balls.

"Yeah, they seem happy together. They're a good match. Odd, but good."

I caressed Clark's warm, heavy balls. After that, I had trouble talking because Clark was moaning into my mouth. He kissed his way down my body, suckled and nibbled on my nipples, dipped his tongue into my belly button, and sucked on my cock. My body quivered and I ran my fingers through his soft hair.

"Feels good, angel. Don't stop."

He sucked for a little longer, then pulled off. I whimpered at the loss, but Clark kissed and licked my balls, which made up for it.

"I want to taste all of you tonight."

His tongue moved over both balls, down my perineum, and inched farther down. My breath hitched in anticipation, I raised my knees up and out to provide him better access, and then...

"Give me a minute. There's something I need to get from the closet."

I groaned and pulled him to me.

"Don't worry, sweetheart. I promise to eat that

gorgeous ass of yours. My mouth is already watering for you. I'll be right back."

Clark hopped off the bed, walked over to the closet, and then returned with a handful of ties. My cock twitched and pearly drops dribbled from my slit. Clark looked at my body appreciatively.

"I'll take that as a yes."

Had he asked me a question? I raised my arms up to the slats on the headboard, hoping that I knew where things were going. Clark confirmed his plan when he secured my wrists to the bed with the ties. Once he had me restrained, he slipped his fingers through the fabric against my wrist.

"Not too tight, are they, sweetheart?"

He was so damn sweet and earnest.

"They're perfect, angel. I feel really good."

A contented sigh left his mouth and his shoulders relaxed.

"Close your eyes."

I immediately obeyed and felt another smooth tie slide along my cheek and across my eyes. Clark secured the blindfold with a loose knot.

"Are you going to gag me too?"

He licked my lips and kissed me.

"Never. I love the sounds you make, love kissing you. No gags."

A shiver ran over my body and Clark's weight lifted off the bed.

"Two minutes. Wait for me."

I pulled on my restraints and chuckled. Like I could go anywhere. It didn't take long for Clark to return and resume his feast on my body. My nipples were suckled, belly button licked, and throat sucked. I relaxed against the bed and let the pleasure of Clark taking care of me wash over my body.

"You make me feel so damn good, angel."

He sucked my balls into his mouth, then pushed my knees forward onto my chest and out to the side. His tongue licked down my balls, over my perineum, and up my cleft. I gasped air into my lungs and clutched the headboard with my hands.

"Oh, Clark, yeah. Lick my hole, fuck my ass with your tongue. Feels so good."

Clark licked my cleft with his flattened tongue, then he pointed it and penetrated me as he stroked my cock. I moaned and pushed my hips up and down to thrust my cock into his warm hand and my asshole onto his wet tongue. Clark's happy groans and sighs mixed with mine, further arousing me. Just as I neared my release, Clark pulled his hand off my dick and his tongue out of my ass. I whimpered in frustration.

I felt his weight leave the bed, heard him walk out of the room, and then return a couple of minutes later. He rejoined me on the bed and kissed me deeply.

"Trying something new, sweetheart. Let me know if you don't like it."

A cold drop of liquid against my thighs and my body

trembled. Then I heard Clark fumble in the nightstand, the sound of the cap on the bottle of lube snapping open, and a thump as it hit the floor.

"Keep your legs pulled up and your knees spread for me, Noah."

Thank goodness for lots of time working out and good flexibility. Still, I hadn't completely recovered from the accident, so holding these types of positions for long wasn't as easy as it used to be. Instead, I planted my feet on the bed and tilted my hips up. That left me spread open for Clark. Well, I expected Clark. Instead, a slick, cold, hard surface touched my pucker. I gasped.

"What is that?"

"Ice dildo. This okay, Noah?"

What the hell? The icy hardness pushed against the ring of muscles in my opening, massaging and then penetrating me. I gasped.

"Cold! 'S so cold."

Clark bent over my body and kissed me, moving his hot tongue in and out of my mouth at the same pace he moved the frozen dildo in and out of my ass. The sensation was uncomfortable at first, but also oddly erotic. After a few strokes, uncomfortable turned into pleasurable. My dick pulsed and leaked against my stomach and my ass opened itself to the invasion.

"More, please. Yes. Oh Christ, fuck me. Yeah."

As my body adjusted to the ice pounding into it, I

became accustomed and somewhat numb to the cold. That was when Clark pulled out the ice dildo and shoved his long, thick, hot dick deep into my chute with one swift motion. The sudden temperature deviation sent tingles all through my channel.

"Ungh!"

"Need you, Noah. Need you so damn much."

He was grunting and pummeling me. I was panting and bucking against him. Harsh sounds of skin slapping against skin filled the air. Over and over again, we moved together, his body in mine, his hand flying on my cock, until I felt Clark tense and spill inside me as I sprayed our chests and stomachs with my seed.

Clark leaned down and suckled my ear. I could feel his heart racing and hear him gasping to get air into his lungs. After several long seconds, he pushed himself off me, removed my blindfold, and released my hands from the bindings. He straddled my body, placed a knee on either side of my torso, and rubbed the parts of my wrists that the ties had touched.

"You okay, sweetheart?"

I pulled him down on top of me and kissed him.

"I'm great. Amazing. Happy. That was fucking hot."

Clark chuckled.

"I was going for cold. Well, hot and cold."

"Mmmm. Goal accomplished. One hot tongue plus one cold ice dildo plus one hot dick equals one happy ass."

Clark's hands moved to my ribs.

"Goofball."

He laughed and tickled me. I joined in and gave barely there touches to his armpits, knowing how that made him jump. We rolled around the bed, smearing cum everywhere and laughing as our hands found each other's sensitive spots and drew out giggles.

"Love you, Noah," Clark gasped out as he lay down and wrapped his arms around me.

"Love you too, angel. Always."

We curled together, tight together, and went to sleep.

I WAS lying in bed watching Clark sleep when I heard a knock at the door. Yes, I was watching him sleep. The man looked beautiful when he was sleeping: his ivory skin relaxed, his cheeks rosy, and he often had a little smile on his red lips. Okay, he pretty much looked like that when he was awake too. What could I say? He took my breath away, really did.

He must have been completely exhausted, because he didn't even budge when the knock came a second time. I scooted out of bed, pulled on a pair of pants, and walked out of the bedroom. I closed the door softly, then rushed down the hallway, through the living room, and over to the entryway so I could answer the door before the knocking got louder and woke Clark up. The only thing keeping me from patting myself on the back for having satisfied Clark into such a state of oblivion that he could sleep through that noise was that my hands were busy pulling on a shirt.

I opened the door, ready to ask whoever it was to keep it down, but then I saw my brother's worried face. Shit! I'd forgotten to call Ben after we left the hospital.

"Hey, come on in."

"Thank God you're here. I've been terrified."

I walked to the kitchen and signaled for him to follow. The kitchen was the room farthest from the bedroom, so we could talk in there without waking Clark. Plus, it was always a safe bet that a conversation with any member of my family would be improved by a liberal addition of alcohol.

"Sorry, man. I came to the door as fast as I could. I'm not running on all cylinders yet, okay?"

I pointed down at my legs. I was actually doing really well. No marathons in my immediate future and I probably couldn't do a butterfly kick, but I'd get there.

Ben caught up with me in the kitchen, reached for me, and pulled me into a tight embrace.

"I wasn't talking about the door, Noah. I've been calling the hospital every few days since you threw me out and they refused to tell me anything. I kept waiting for you to get your damn memory back and call me, but you never did. So today I went down there, thinking I'd sneak into your room, but I couldn't find you and then they told me you weren't a patient anymore."

He pushed me out of the hug and held my shoulders

as he glared at me.

"I thought you died, asshole. Don't do that to me. You're my brother and I love you. Don't shut me out, Noah."

I shoved him off me, walked over to the refrigerator, and got us each a beer.

"Simmer down, Suzie Q. I'm fine. No need to get your ruffled panties in a twirl. I thought I was supposed to be the fairy Forman, not you."

I handed him his beer and sat down. Ben rolled his eyes.

"You're not a fairy, Noah."

"Don't get all PC on me now, big brother. I remember all the words you've used over the years. You probably still do, you've just stopped saying them in front of the pink sheep of the family."

Ben chuckled.

"Oh, come on, Noah. You're not gay."

He was relaxed in his chair, nursing his beer. I thought he was kidding around, so I laughed, flipped my chair around, and straddled it.

"Huh. Well, if you're sure. But I don't know how else to explain the mouth-dick-ass combo that goes on in this house."

Okay, that might have sounded a little crass, but I was still groggy from sleep. That was the first beer I'd had in a hell of a long time, I'd already chugged it down, and frankly, I'd never had a good censor when it came to my mouth.

Ben looked a bit nervous, but then he smirked.

"You had me going there for a second, Noah. I almost believed you."

"Well, everybody needs to believe in something. And I believe I'll have another beer." I got up and walked to the fridge. "You want one?"

"Nah, I'm good, still working on this one. But seriously, Noah, maybe it's time you got a steady girlfriend. Blaire has a friend who's like a nine or a nine and a half on scale of one to ten. Do you want me to set you up?"

I looked into my brother's eyes and realized that he was actually serious.

"Christ, Ben! On a scale of one to ten, you're a complete asshole."

Ben looked at me in confusion.

"What? What did I say?"

Honestly, some people should be court-ordered to have a Breathalyzer connected to their voice box.

"Ben, you haven't finished even one beer and you just tried to set me up with a woman."

"So? Why can't you have someone steady? What's wrong with that?"

"Ben! I do have someone steady, the same someone for almost a decade. You know, that's like ten *years* as opposed to your lifetime relationship record, which I think is about ten *days*."

"Hey! I've been with Blaire for almost three weeks."

"In a world full of generic people, you, my friend, are

a designer brand."

I shook my head at him in disbelief, then decided the best course of action was to change the subject.

"Look, I'm sorry you were worried. When I woke up in the hospital, I'd blocked out the last three hellish years of my life, so my memory of you wasn't exactly shiny-happy, you know? As far as I remembered, we weren't exactly on speaking terms. I only just remembered everything when Clark clued me in."

Ben's head snapped up.

"Clark? You...you talked with Clark? When did you talk with Clark?"

I saw trepidation, or maybe fear, in his eyes. What the hell was that about?

CHAPTER NINETEEN

Noah—Present

I WAS wondering what'd made my brother get all worked up when we heard a noise and turned toward the door to see the man of the hour in the flesh. Literally. Clark must have shuffled out of bed to look for me without realizing we had company. That was my guess, anyway, because he was stark naked, rubbing the sleep from his eyes, and looking delicious. I was torn between wanting to cover him up so that nobody else could see his stunning body and wanting to lick him from head to toe.

Ben's jaw dropped when he saw Clark. He stared at him openly with a look that had to be shock and then he jumped backward with such force that he knocked his chair to the ground. Clark looked up when he heard the noise, turned a deep scarlet, and walked out of the kitchen, mumbling about being right back. Ben hadn't taken his eyes off Clark, and when he turned around to leave the kitchen, Ben started shaking.

My brother looked like he was having a nervous breakdown, and Clark had left the kitchen to go get dressed.

That meant I was stuck handling Ben.

"Ben? What the hell? Are you okay?"

I got up and adjusted my hard dick. Hey, naked Clark, remember? Front and back view. That was like a recipe for insta-hard-on, no additional ingredients necessary.

"H-h-h-he was..."

At that point I thought there was a real possibility that my brother was on something. He was shaking and pale. His eyes were unfocused and petrified. And, oddly, he had a raging hard-on. Hmm. I'd seen Viagra in Ben's medicine cabinet once. Maybe somebody spiked it with mushrooms. I took a deep breath and walked toward him slowly.

Ben swallowed hard, then looked at me.

"I thought he moved away."

"Only because he thought that's what I wanted. But he loves me, so he came back."

I had almost reached my brother when he rushed past me so fast that I fell against the counter. I caught myself and looked up just in time to see Ben reaching his fist in the air and Clark, now dressed in jeans and pulling on a T-shirt, bracing himself for impact.

Okay, I was injured, but not dead, and no fucking way was anyone going to touch my angel. I leaped across the floor and landed a solid, spinning backfist that had Ben on his knees, clutching his nose with one hand and his ear with the other. I was ready to follow up with an eye slap when Clark stepped in between my arms and pressed his body against mine.

"Noah, stop. Please don't fight with your brother about me. Please, sweetheart. I don't want you to do this."

All the rage left my body. There was no room for anger when I had Clark. I ran my hands over his neck and face to check for damage. My brother hadn't actually connected any blows, but I needed to be sure. Needed to feel that Clark was unharmed. I touched his nose, his cheeks, his eyes. Then I covered him with kisses.

"What about what I want?"

We both looked down at Ben on the ground. He had moved his hands off his face, but he was still crouched on his knees and he was looking up at Clark.

"We were best friends for years, roommates. I thought we were there for each other. I thought we...we loved each other too."

My brother looked so lost that I actually felt sorry for him. We'd already been over the whole betrayal he'd felt when he'd thought his friend had seduced his brother, which had been his immediate reaction when I'd told him I was in love with Clark. I'd explained it to him enough times back then. Told him I was the damn instigator of the relationship. Explained that Clark didn't make me gay. Yes, I actually had to spell that out for Ben. Don't ask me how Mister Magna-cum-laude couldn't figure that shit out for himself.

I came out to my brother when I graduated from college. I'd waited until then because it was easier to lie and have my parents pay for school than tell the truth and be saddled with student loans for the rest of my life. Yeah, it was pathetic. But Clark convinced me that I was being fiscally responsible.

It wasn't like it mattered all that much. Clark and I lived together in the same one-bedroom apartment all through my college years. He only had one year of school left when I got to State, but he stayed after he graduated and worked. My family thought we were roommates, just like he'd been with Ben. We never let them visit, of course, but that wasn't too hard to accomplish because Ben never asked and my parents didn't mind so long as we went to see them for holidays.

State was only a little more than an hour away from EC North, the suburb where my parents lived, so we'd make day trips and split the time between my family and Clark's aunt and uncle's family. My parents had always liked Clark; they felt sorry for him because he had lost his mother, so they let him join us for holiday meals. The plus side of that was that we were together; the downside was that we couldn't touch each other. We usually made up for it when we got to his aunt's house. Poor Shirley had to constantly clear her throat to remind us that there were other people in the room.

Anyway, after I graduated and was no longer dependent on my parents in any way, I was ready to tell them. For some reason, Clark thought it'd be easier to start with Ben. He was sure my brother would be accepting, and then I'd have an ally when I told my parents. I expected all three of them to freak out and disown me, so it didn't matter to me which one of them got the first shot in.

Unfortunately, Clark had been overly optimistic about my brother's reaction. When I explained that I was gay and Clark and I were moving to EC West together, Ben went crazy. He told all of the guys he and Clark had hung out with in college, which resulted in years of loneliness for Clark until he finally managed to get a few of them to listen to him and then they sort of reconnected.

After that, I refused to talk with Ben unless he apologized to Clark, and he couldn't have a conversation with me without insulting the man I'd thought was his best friend, so that was that. I wrote him off for two years until that fateful day when he somehow managed to talk me into being the biggest fucking piece of shit asshole on the planet. But you've already heard that story.

ANYWAY, AFTER the horrible night when I had driven Clark away, Ben told me he understood how I felt about Clark and he was sorry. When he'd said that, I'd honestly believed that he *finally* accepted his brother was gay. As a result, we'd had a fairly decent relationship since then.

"Your friendship meant a lot to him, Ben. But you can't expect him to give me up to save it. Just like I wasn't willing to give him up. You just tried to set me up with a woman, so

I see that this whole gay thing is confusing to you for some unfathomable reason, but try to understand that the way you feel about Clark and the way I feel about Clark just aren't the same. We're in love with each other. Why can't you get that, Ben?"

Ben stood up and looked at Clark through teary eyes.

"You didn't tell him."

I suddenly realized that Clark had been unusually quiet throughout the entire exchange in the kitchen. Then he answered Ben.

"It wasn't mine to tell."

Ben slumped into a seat at the table. I picked up the chair that he had knocked down earlier, sat in it all the way back, spread my knees, and pulled Clark onto the chair, between my legs. His body stiffened, which had never happened in response to my touch. He softened quickly and melted back against me, but not before I saw the look of discomfort on his face and noticed that my brother wouldn't look at us.

"What in the hell is going on? What didn't Clark tell me?"

Ben shifted in his seat and stared at the table with such intensity I wondered whether he was trying to find a way to burn a hole through it.

"My chances of getting you to let this go are..."

"A few degrees lower than hell freezing over and a couple of miles south of hopeless. Now speak, Ben."

My brother lifted his hand to his nose and poked it tenderly. I rolled my eyes at him.

"Oh, come on. It isn't that bad, Ben. It's not like I broke it or anything."

"I think maybe you did. Why'd you hit me so hard?"

I decided against the truth—that the second I saw my angel threatened I was filled with such rage that I saw fucking red and I wanted to kill the person responsible, even if it was my brother. So, instead, I wrapped my arms around Clark, rested my head on his shoulder, and waggled my eyebrows at my brother.

"Hey, you were aiming for his mouth. I have a vested interest in making sure that particular body part is in full working order."

"Noah, don't."

Clark's voice held a warning tone I didn't understand. Ben was refusing to say anything, just shifting in his seat uncomfortably. Something was going on, but I couldn't figure out what it was. I decided my best chance of getting an answer was reading Clark's face. We knew each other so well we didn't need words to communicate. A skill that came in handy in crowded parties and in bed, and one I knew we hadn't lost during our time apart, just like we hadn't lost our connection. Never would.

"Get up for a minute would you, angel?"

I patted Clark's back as I spoke. He jumped right out of the chair and looked down at me, concern etched all over his handsome face.

"You okay, sweetheart? Did I hurt your legs?"

I laughed and stroked his thigh.

"Angel, if straddling you hurt me in a bad way, we'd have a huge fucking problem. Literally."

Clark's eyes shot over to Ben and a concerned expression took over his face. Then he straightened his shoulders back and looked determinedly at my brother.

"It's time for you to talk to your brother, Ben. We go back a long way. You were a good friend to me for a lot of years and I truly do love you."

I growled and dug my fingers into Clark's thighs. He bent down, kissed my neck, and stroked my belly. The tension started draining from my body, but not before Ben noticed my reaction.

"Jesus, Noah. What in the hell is wrong with you?"

Clark continued petting me while he responded to my brother.

"Nothing is wrong with him. He's just a bit possessive and he doesn't like hearing me say that I love anybody other than him."

My angel looked into my eyes and combed his fingers through my hair.

"Even though he knows it isn't the same kind of love. He knows it never could be with anybody else because he's always been everything to me."

I loved that he was still unfazed by my jealousy and

used to explaining why his partner turned into a rabid wolf at the slightest indication that someone was even thinking about coming close to its mate. It was clear that those years apart had done nothing to take away our familiarity with each other. Clark didn't stop touching me, but he raised his head toward my brother as he kept talking.

"He told me what you said to him back then, that you pushed him to bring that other guy into our apartment and set me up to catch him. He was wrong to do it and I was a complete fool for leaving. But you played a role in it, Ben."

I could hear Clark's voice shaking and feel his fingers trembling. I wrapped my arms around his waist and rested my head against his stomach, hoping to give him comfort.

"I can't tell you how much I wish he'd done it for another reason. Boredom, experimentation, even thinking I was a bad lay. Any of the million reasons I'd thought about during the last three years of sleepless nights would've been better than the one reason I hadn't ever considered—your betrayal. He's your brother and you two need to be a part of each other's lives. I've always encouraged Noah to do that. But let me be very clear about this with you. I will not lose him again, Ben. Not for a single minute. I'm not walking away. Now you tell him why you did it or I will."

When I saw the look in Clark's eyes as he stared Ben down across the kitchen table, the pieces all finally fell together. In that moment, I knew. I fucking knew what had happened. A wave of jealousy washed over me and a roar left my throat as my body shook. I clenched my fist and lunged at my brother. I was going to fucking rip his throat out.

Ben shot me a panicked look and Clark laid his hand on my chest with the lightest touch imaginable.

"He's your brother, Noah. Your *brother*. Sit down, sweetheart. Please sit down."

I clasped his shoulders and pulled him behind me to shield him from Ben, then wound my arms backward and held him against my back. Ben's mouth was hanging open as he watched us. Clark stroked my cheek, extricated himself from my embrace, sat in the chair, and pulled me down to sit between his spread legs, so that he was behind me and I was looking at my brother. Okay, shooting daggers with my eyes at him, but that was a type of look, right?

Ben had his lips pursed and he refused to speak, so Clark did.

"Okay, fine. I'll tell him."

I kept my eyes on my brother.

"You don't have to tell me, angel. I figured it out. He came on to you."

CHAPTER TWENTY

Noah—Present

BEN'S HEAD shot up when I accused him of coming on to Clark. Panicked words spilled out of his mouth in a rush.

"No, I didn't, not really, umm..."

At that point, I'd had enough. I was barely holding it together. I covered my eyes with my hands and whispered to Clark, "I don't like being left out of this. What happened between the two of you and when did it happen?"

Clark kissed my neck and wrapped his arms around me. I could feel his heart beating against my back and his breath under my ear. His earthy, vanilla scent filled me, keeping me calm. And because he had positioned us so that I was between him and my brother, I was able to muster enough restraint to remain in that chair and off my brother.

"Remember when he got back from his graduation trip to Europe and he wanted to go out one last time before he left for grad school in Chicago?"

Clark and I were already living together by then. Had been for a couple of months. I didn't like where this story was going. I started shaking and sweating.

"Shhh, sweetheart. It wasn't serious. He got drunk, really drunk, and he, umm, he tried to kiss me and, ehm, touch me, but I pushed him away and *nothing* happened. I promise."

Ben jumped in, a terrified look on his face.

"I'm not gay!"

I yelled at my brother.

"Are you going to say it didn't happen, Ben? Are you actually going to call Clark a liar?"

"No, I didn't say that. It happened, but I'm not gay!"

I noticed Ben hadn't denied putting the moves on Clark. So my brother was gay. I supposed that was one explanation for his maniacal need to be in a relationship with a woman constantly and the fact that not a one of those relationships lasted longer than a tube of toothpaste.

"Fine. You're not gay. You just tried to make out with another man. Totally straight behavior as far as I'm concerned. Whatever. Just tell me what the master plan was, Ben. If you couldn't have him for yourself, then no one else could either? Is that why you talked me into cheating on him? I don't know how I never saw it before."

"No! Of course not. I did it to save you from him! I'd tried talking to you, reasoning with you, but you're so damn stubborn that nothing worked. Clark had you convinced that you were in love with him. If I didn't step in, you'd never have gotten away from him."

I rolled my eyes at that statement.

"Jesus, Ben, do you ever just, you know, get sick of yourself? Why would I want to get away from him?"

"Because you can't have a life with him, Noah! You'll never be able to get married, never have kids, never have a real family. You won't be able to get the same kind of jobs as normal people. Won't have friends. Everyone will look at you when you walk down the street and they'll *know* what you do with him. The only way for you to have a normal life is to get away from Clark. Trust me on this. I did it myself and it worked."

His eyes were wild and he was waving his hands as he spoke. I understood that he wasn't really talking about me. He was just verbalizing the internal dialogue that probably played on a loop in his head.

"Wow. You open your mouth and the crazy just pours right out."

"What? It's true!"

"Ben, I'm gay. I was gay before I met Clark. I was gay when he was gone these past few years. And I'll be gay for the rest of my life. I have friends. I have a good job. He has given me the most *real* family I've ever had. And I don't give a shit if people I pass by on the street know what I do with him. But I can tell you that it's very unlikely their imagination comes anywhere close to what we actually share, and there's no way they can grasp how fucking good it feels."

Clark's voice came over my shoulder.

"Noah, take it easy."

"Why should I take it easy? I get that he doesn't want to think about you with another man, but are you hearing this bullshit?"

I turned back to my brother.

"You get to win the most-pathetically-overcompensating-homo-of-the-year award, Ben. Do you actually fuck all those pretty little girlfriends or are they just beards so you can keep your sorry ass in the closet? What's the long-term plan here, big brother? You going to marry one of them, live a nice little life on the outside while you slowly die on the inside? Or maybe you'll run off to the bathhouses or bars to get some man-on-man action on the side? Hey, if we're lucky, we can read the tell-all book when your wife leaves you after the kids are grown. Does that sound like a *normal* life to you, Ben?"

My brother had never seen Clark and me together as a couple. He was in graduate school out of state by the time we truly got together, so we only saw him during holidays, when we made day trips to my parents' house. I'd always wondered why Ben and Clark didn't talk on the phone and why Ben never pushed to spend time with his friend on those rare occasions when he visited my parents. But I hadn't given it much thought, because it had helped hide the nature of our relationship from my family.

Then, around the same time Ben graduated and moved back to Emile City, I came out and we didn't see each other for an entirely different reason. I had thought it was because my brother couldn't deal with the fact that Clark and I were gay. As it turned out, dealing with his feelings and the idea of Clark and me as a couple was what had gotten to him.

Ben's face was pale and he looked completely defeated, but I just couldn't find a way to feel sorry for him. He was choosing this torture by denying who he was and I simply couldn't respect that. Plus, he wanted Clark. My Clark. I thought about all the years that Ben and Clark had been friends, about the years they'd lived together. Had my brother been checking him out that entire time? Looking at his body, drooling after his dick, finding excuses to rub up against him?

A growl I couldn't control left my body. I turned around in the chair, straddled Clark's body, and ground my dick against his. That immediately caused my cock to fill and I felt a responding hardness. That was satisfying, but not enough. I needed more. I needed to show Ben that Clark belonged to me.

I pressed my mouth over Clark's in a desperate kiss and claimed him once again. I licked and sucked as my body trembled and my head pounded. *Mine. Mine. Mine.* When we finally separated in order to find some oxygen, Clark's lips were swollen and he was panting and trembling.

"Nobody else touches you. Nobody else fucking looks at you. I don't care if he's my brother. You're mine."

Clark molded himself to me, rubbed my sides, and made a soft "shhhh" sound in my ear.

"Of course, I'm yours. Nobody else's. Don't want

anybody but you. I've *never* wanted anybody but you, Noah."

That calmed me down some, but I still turned and glared at my brother, feeling no mercy.

"He's *mine*."

"Noah, he's just having a hard time coming to terms with who he is, and I was the guy he spent the most time with. He doesn't want me. Not really. He never has. He was confused about his desire for men in general, so he projected those feelings on the closest candidate."

Clark believed what he was saying, because Clark never did understand how beautiful he was, how desirable. People we didn't know turned their heads to look at his alabaster skin, his strawberry-blond hair, his crystal-blue eyes, and his sinewy body as he passed by on the street. But it was more than just his appearance that drew people to Clark. He was warm, funny, confident, and smart. Every one of our friends would have pushed me aside and jumped at the chance to be with him. Well, they'd have tried anyway; I'd have kicked their fucking asses.

I could only imagine what it must have been like for my brother to be so close to Clark all those years without truly possessing him. If Ben was gay, which was pretty clear to me at that point, it must have been fucking torture. And to have Clark minimize the reality of Ben's feelings, well, I'd hated having him do the same thing to me when he'd thought I was a kid with a silly crush. To hear that as a grown man who had been carrying a torch for close to half his life had to be unbearable.

Damn it. I felt sorry for Ben. Actually ached for my brother. He wasn't a bad guy, really. He had been a good friend to Clark. And he had always tried to take care of me, even when I was a real prick. Yeah, the bullshit stunt he had pulled a few years prior damn near killed all of us, but Clark was right—Ben wasn't the only one responsible. We had all played a role, and I was the damn lead.

Plus, I believed my brother truly thought he'd done it to save me. He'd been in love with Clark for so long that he probably justified his feelings by telling himself that they were limited to one man. When I told him Clark and I were together, he probably assumed I'd fallen under a similar spell.

"Clark, don't say that, okay?"

He furrowed his brow and looked at me.

"Ben might have been confused about his feelings toward men, but that doesn't change how he felt..." I swallowed, stuffed the growl that wanted to come out back into my throat, and clenched and released my fists. "Or still feels about you. It's not fair to him to belittle those feelings."

I was looking at Clark as I spoke, so I didn't see Ben's face. But I did hear him. It started as a whimper, moved to a cry, and ended with my brother holding his face in his hands and sobbing while we sat around the kitchen table.

What do you say to your "thirty-one-year-old and just finally owned that he's gay" brother? Hell, how do you even know whether he *has* finally owned it? I don't have the answers to those questions. Clark told Ben that he was still his friend, that we were both there for him, that we loved him, and that we'd listen when he was ready to talk. I didn't punch Ben out when Clark gave him a light hug as he was leaving our house. All in all, I'd say we both showed extreme compassion.

After Ben left, Clark and I stood together and stared at the door. I wondered whether Clark had ever had an interest in my brother, whether they'd have ended up together if I hadn't been in the picture.

"No way, no how."

I turned my head to him.

"Did I just say that out loud?"

"No, but I know what you were thinking. Ben is wonderful, but he isn't my type. I can honestly tell you that I have *never* thought of him as anything other than a friend. Of course, his being your brother would have stopped anything anyway, but it never got to that point because, with you around or not, Ben and I were never going to happen."

I was skeptical.

"He's cute. Really cute. Okay, let's face it, he's more than cute. I mean, come on—his body, his face. Ben's seriously hot."

Clark laughed and hugged me.

"Sweetheart, I'm not turned on by the whole incest thing, so let's slow down on the 'my brother is hot' talk, okay? Besides, I'm not blind. I know what Ben looks like. But he doesn't do it for me."

I sucked on his neck and ran my hands up his arm in a touch so light it was more like a tickle.

"Oh yeah? Who does it for you?"

Clark moaned and walked me backward to our bedroom.

"A guy who can kick my ass, but wants to save it instead."

He sucked on my neck so hard I was sure he'd added another mark, then pulled off my shirt and pants.

"A guy who is so rough, people cross to the other side of the street to avoid getting in his way, but who turns into a marshmallow when we're alone together."

He took off his clothes, kissed me breathless, then sat on the edge of the bed.

"A guy who stands tall and proud when he faces the world, but falls to his knees when he's facing me."

I moaned, dropped to my knees, and took his long, hot, hard cock into my mouth. That was nothing like a dildo. I'd even bought one I thought was around the same size as Clark, just so I could pretend, you know? But that thing had just given me a sore jaw. The real tool was smooth as velvet, warm, and tasted of sweat and sex and *Clark*.

"A guy who hasn't needed anything from his parents

or anyone else since before he was a teenager, but who needs everything from me and has from day one."

He pulled my mouth off his dick and lifted me to my feet. Then he lowered me onto the bed on my back and crawled on top of me. He looked into my eyes and kissed each of my cheeks in turn.

"A guy whose face seems harsh and tough when he looks at other people, but is soft and adoring when he looks at me."

He ran his fingers down my chest and stomach, then over to my cock. He stroked me a few times and caressed my balls.

"A guy who has his own mind and knows how to use it, but chooses to defer to mine."

He got the lube from the nightstand, covered his fingers, and rubbed it into my opening. I pushed down against his fingers, dying for a ride.

"A guy who hasn't ever cared what anyone else thinks, but hangs on my every word."

He gave me a heart-pounding, brain-melting kiss. I whimpered, clung to his back, and lifted my knees up and wrapped my ankles around his back.

"A guy who I fell in love with before I even understood what that meant."

Then he was sliding into me, stretching me wide open, and we both lost the power of speech. There were hands rubbing and tugging, mouths moaning and kissing, and hips pounding and snapping.

I planted my feet on the mattress and arched my back so I could use every ounce of power I had to meet his thrusts. My body was on fire, consumed by the knowledge that, after having been denied its master for all those years, it was finally being reclaimed, possessed, owned.

"Soon, Noah."

Clark grunted into my ear while he slammed his dick into my ass and pulled on my cock. Over and over. In and out. So damn deep, so fucking hard, and so incredibly good.

"Uh-huh. Uh-huh. Uh-huh."

No words, just sounds. I was getting everything I needed, everything I'd craved and dreamed of over the previous three years. Speaking was way beyond my abilities in that moment.

"Now, Noah."

I could feel his dick pulsing inside me as he grasped my ass with one hand and pulled in tight while he continued tugging on my cock with his other hand.

"Oh!"

My body immediately reacted by releasing thick ropes of cum over my stomach and chest. We lay against each other, gasping and touching. By the time my heart rate slowed and I was finally able to breathe and think enough to speak, I was too overwhelmed with emotion.

"Oh, angel. I don't know what to say."

"How about a kiss instead of words? I love your kisses."

Now that I could do. Again and again, for the rest of my life.

THE END

(BUT WAIT…THERE'S MORE—BONUS CHAPTER AHEAD.)

BONUS CHAPTER

When the U.S. Supreme Court released their historic marriage decision, I wanted to celebrate so I wrote a bonus chapter with Noah and Clark's reaction to the wonderful news. I hope you enjoy it. –CC

PEOPLE SAY time flies. They say you blink and suddenly years have passed. Not me. I turned thirty this year, and when I look back at my life and the world when I was twenty, it seems like way longer than millions of blinks. Ten years ago, I was in college, living with the only man I'd ever loved, the only man I'd ever wanted, and feeling frustrated that I had to hide our relationship from my family. Today, I'm still with that man, I still love him with everything I am, and I've still never, not once, wanted anybody else.

"MORNING, NOAH," Clark whispered from behind me. He kissed his way down the numbers tattooed on the back of my neck, wrapped his arm around my waist, and caressed my chest and belly.

I reached back, massaged his hip and ass, and said, "Morning, angel. How'd you sleep?"

"Good." Clark kissed a path across my shoulder.

I rolled onto my back, pulled him onto my chest, and pushed his strawberry-blond hair off his forehead. "You came to bed really late."

Clark had his own computer consulting company, focusing mostly on security. His clients were located all over the world, which meant that though he worked from home most of the time, his schedule wasn't nine-to-five. Plus, he was so good at what he did that over the past few years, demand for his services had grown to the point that he could work all day, every day, if that was what he wanted. Not that his success was any surprise; Clark was brilliant. And I was damn proud of him.

"Yeah, everyone else on that conference call was in Hong Kong, so the time change made it hard." He kissed my chest and tangled his legs with mine. "I didn't wake you up when I came in, did I?"

"No. I just don't sleep well unless you're in bed with me." I combed my fingers through his soft hair. "So I was sort of in and out."

Clark licked at my nipple. "Sorry, sweetheart."

"'S okay. Mmm, feels good," I rasped.

He suckled the now-hard bud, then reached for my groin and fondled my balls. Every so often, he'd massage the area beneath them and dip a long finger into my crease.

"Are you going to fuck me, angel?" I asked him.

"Don't know yet," he answered, and then he licked my

hard shaft from root to crown. "I think I'll suck you for now and then decide."

"'Kay," I said as I spread my legs and relaxed, enjoying the feeling of Clark's touch.

Clark circled his hand around the base of my dick and sucked the head into his mouth. It felt amazing—the friction, the heat, all his attention focused only on me. After a couple of minutes, Clark popped his mouth off, though he kept stroking me with one hand and massaging my balls, perineum, and ass with the other.

"I love how you listen to me," he said. "You'll do whatever I say, won't you?" His voice was rough with arousal.

I met Clark's gaze and answered without hesitation, "Always. Anything you want, angel." He moved two fingers down my crease and pressed the tips into my hole, making me buck and gasp. "Anything," I said again, barely audible this time.

He beamed and said, "You're beautiful, Noah. So beautiful." Then he dipped down and sucked me into his mouth again, moving faster, stroking harder, and pushing his fingers in deeper.

"Yes," I moaned and tilted my hips up, trying to make myself even more accessible to this man who had owned me from the day I climbed in through my childhood bedroom window and first laid eyes on him. "So good, Clark. So good."

A few more sucks and then he was crawling up the bed. "On your side," he said. I rolled onto my left side and Clark fit himself behind me. "Right knee forward, sweetheart."

I let him position me however he wanted and sighed in pleasure when I felt his slick fingers circle around my puckered entrance. It didn't take long before he was gripping my hip and pushing his way into my body with his thick, perfect cock. I moaned when he bottomed out.

"Good?" he whispered into my ear as he slid his hand across my belly and cupped my balls.

"It's always good with us. Whenever we're together," I added. "It's good."

"Yeah." His hot breath on my ear made me shiver, and his hand wrapping around my dick and stroking made me cry out his name. "It sure is."

We stopped talking then and moved in concert, enjoying the feeling of each other's body, each other's scent. As he slid his shaft in and out of my hole, Clark kissed, nibbled, and sucked on my neck and shoulders and stroked my dick. He grunted and I moaned as we moved faster and faster until Clark finally rolled me onto my belly and started jackhammering into me.

"Clark!" I yelled as I arched my neck and tried to get used to this harder, faster invasion.

"I'm almost there," he said roughly as he tangled the fingers of one hand in my hair, pulling hard, and clasped my shoulder with the other, holding me in place. "Almost there."

True to his prediction, he moved his dick in and out of my body a few more times and then he shoved in as deep as he could and stilled, shooting into me and crying out my name. As soon as he was done, Clark flipped me onto my back, fisted my cock, and started jacking me off.

"Come on," he said as he moved his free hand to my balls and squeezed them. "Give it to me, Noah." He moved his hand in a rapid massage over my balls, perineum, and crease. "Come on, come on, come—"

"Oh God, yes!" I bucked hard and came even harder, streaking my body with the evidence of my pleasure.

Clark collapsed on top of me and sighed in satisfaction. I kissed the top of his head and did the same.

"Thank you, angel," I said.

"My pleasure, sweetheart."

OKAY, SO I've told you about the parts of my life that are the same. Now for the differences from a decade ago: I'm done with school; I own a small kickboxing gym; my parents know exactly who Clark is to me and that he comes first, always and in all things; and my brother, Ben, is a big part of my life. I still give him a hard time every so often, old habits die hard and all that, but the truth is, I genuinely like Ben and his family.

"HEY, NOAH," Micah Trains said as he walked into my gym

that afternoon.

"Micah! What are you doing here?"

Micah gave me a crooked grin and raised one eyebrow. "Thanks for the welcome, Mr. Congeniality."

I flipped him off and said, "Fuck you."

He'd opened his mouth to respond when his phone rang. "Can't leave the office for five fucking minutes, I swear," he muttered as he pulled his phone out of his suit pocket. Then he looked up at me and said, "I have to take this. Sorry. I'll be fast."

"No problem. Let's walk to my office. It's quieter."

My office wasn't anything fancy like the law firm where Micah and my brother, Ben, worked, but it was good enough to meet my needs and it had a door that closed, which kept out the bulk of the noise.

"'Lo." Micah followed me to the back as he answered his phone. "Yeah, I got his e-mail." Pause. "No fucking way in hell am I settling the case, Janet."

I opened my office door and held my arm out in invitation. Micah walked inside.

"Because your guy absconded with down payments from over fifty investors and he needs to pay them back, with interest, or give up the parcels of land." Another pause. "No, your associate's e-mail did not contain any new information that's going to change my mind. Frankly, I'm not convinced he actually graduated from law school. Is he the one who worked up this case for you? Because his e-mail was about as coherent as your client's defense, which is to say it makes no sense whatsoever."

I winced. Micah worshiped the ground my brother walked on, and he melted at the sight of his children, but in his professional capacity the man scared the shit out of me. And I did not scare easily.

"I'm not being an asshole, Janet, I'm trying to help you out here. Did you even read his e-mail?" Pause. "Well, you should, because that shit has your firm name on it and he uses no deductive reasoning, capital letters, or punctuation. I wrote him back and asked if he was related to E.E. Cummings, and do you know what he said? He told me that he just moved here from Florida, so none of his relatives live nearby."

At that point, I had to cover my mouth to keep from laughing.

"This is a twenty-five million dollar case, and you need to start treating it that way instead of letting kindergartners who claim to have graduate degrees waste my time with drivel. Either you step in and give your client competent representation, or send that kid you've hired back to school until he can, at a minimum, adhere to the basic rules of English grammar!"

Micah sat down in an empty chair as he nodded. "Okay. I'm glad we understand each other." Pause. "Yeah, dinner at your house next week should be fine. I'll check with Ben and get back to you with a date. My best to Harold and the kids."

He slipped his phone into his pocket, took a deep

breath, and rolled his neck. "Sorry about that. One of my old friends is opposing counsel on a case and we needed to work through some things."

"You're friends with that person?" I asked incredulously.

"Yeah." Micah looked surprised by my tone and question. "Janet and I go way back. Plus, I worked with her husband for years at my old firm. Why do you ask?"

I was afraid to know how he'd deal with someone he didn't like. "No reason," I said with a chuckle. "So what brings you here in the middle of the day?"

"I wanted to see if you and Clark could watch the kids tonight."

We spent a fair bit of time with my niece and nephew, usually with Ben and Micah present, but we'd also done our share of babysitting.

"Sure. You have a business dinner or something?"

"No. And, actually, I was hoping for an overnight deal if you guys can swing it. I can bring them to you, but if you wouldn't mind crashing in our guest room, that'd be easier. They have all their gear and food and cribs and all that."

Well, this was new. We hadn't ever watched the kids for longer than a few hours, not that it was a hardship. Lilah and Raphi were damn cute.

"Yeah, sure thing. You know we love spending time with them. And staying at your house isn't a problem, either. What's going on?"

Micah rose from his seat and tugged on his sleeves to straighten his starched shirt. "You've seen the news, Noah." He met my gaze, and his blue eyes shone. "I'm sure you can figure out what I'm planning, but the first time I say the words, it's going to be to your brother." He walked over to my office door and turned the knob. "If you guys can get there by five thirty or six, that'd be great."

"Will do." I smiled broadly. "And Micah?" He paused and looked back at me over his shoulder. "Congratulations. My brother's a pretty lucky guy."

"I'm the lucky one," Micah said as he walked out the door.

WE HAD just finished bath time and were putting on the twins' pajamas when Ben's home phone rang.

"I've got the little ones," Clark said. "You get the phone."

I smacked a kiss on Clark's lips, squeezed his ass, and then jogged into the kitchen.

"Yellow!" I said in a singsong voice.

Spending an evening with my niece and nephew had put me in a goofy, jovial mood. Well, the company was part of what put me in that mood. Truth be told, I'd left most of the depression that had plagued my teenage and young adult years behind me long ago. These days, when I took stock of my life, I was damn happy with what I saw—good friends, a job I enjoyed, a caring family in the way of my brother and his brood, and the man I'd always wanted standing beside me for all of it. What's not to smile about?

"Noah?" my mother said. "Is that you? I thought I called Ben."

There was a time when her voice, or my father's, would have been enough to make me spin into a rage. But years of radio silence from me, followed by a period of time when my brother's relationship with my parents became equally strained, had made them turn over a new leaf. Either that, or they now kept their disapproval to themselves. Whatever the case, it was no longer miserable to be around them.

"You did," I responded. "Ben and Micah are out tonight. Clark and I are watching the kids until tomorrow."

"Oh," she said, sounding surprised. "He didn't say anything to me about this last time we spoke. It must have come up suddenly. Is everything okay?"

I froze and ran over my options in my mind. I could brush her off, say everything was fine, and let my brother share the news next time he spoke with her. But even though our parents had come a long way, I wasn't sure whether they'd come far enough to be happy about hearing that their son was going to marry a man.

Unlike me, Ben had always sought out our parents' approval, and though I knew their opinions no longer mattered to him at the same level they once had, he would be sad if he met with disapproval in response to what should be a happy announcement. With that thought in mind, I decided that giving my mom and dad a bit of time to absorb the news was worth stealing Ben's thunder.

"Everything is fine, Mom." Just then, Clark walked into the room with Raphi on one hip and Lilah on the other, and I remembered that I wasn't the only one with a happy life. My brother was doing great. "Actually, it's more than fine. The Supreme Court overturned DOMA, so Ben and Micah are out celebrating." I paused and took a deep breath. "They're getting engaged tonight."

Dead silence on the other line. It was better than yelling and carrying on about unnatural behavior, though, so instead of hanging up, I waited for my mother to respond.

"Who is that?" Clark asked as he walked up to me.

I tucked the phone under my ear and reached for Lilah. Clark handed her over, kissed my cheek, and put his hand on my hip.

"It's my mom," I said, and then I took a deep breath and braced myself for the possibility of a fight or a lecture. "Mom? Are you still there?"

After only a brief hesitation, she answered, sounding only a little strained. "Yes, I'm here. That's wonderful news, Noah. I'll make sure to send flowers."

I sighed in relief. "That's nice. I'll let Ben know you called, okay? Say hi to Dad."

"I will. Please give Clark my best. Bye, dear," she said

and then the line went dead.

I set the phone down and dropped my forehead onto Clark's shoulder. He nudged my shirt out of the way, rubbed his fingers over my skin in a soothing caress, and said, "Well?"

"It's a brave new world," I answered and raised my face up so I could look into his eyes.

He snorted. "It sure is. So are your parents going to be okay with this?"

"My parents don't get to have an opinion," I snapped. "It's Ben's life." Clark raised one eyebrow, and I took in a breath. "But, yeah, they'll be fine."

"Good." Clark kissed my neck. "What about you?"

"What about me?"

Clark looked at me meaningfully. "Say the word and I'm there, Noah. You know that, right?"

I cupped his cheek. "I know, angel, but there's nothing any judge or priest or government can say that changes what we are to each other." I shrugged. "Who knows? Maybe someday I'll want to get hitched. But for now? I don't want anybody putting their nose in our relationship. What we have is nobody's business but ours."

He turned his head and kissed my palm. "Works for me, sweetheart."

OKAY, SO to summarize the ten-year life-progress checklist:

done with school, successful business, decent relationship with parents, good relationship with brother, amazing relationship with Clark. I know none of those things may sound like much in the way of drastic differences, but that's because all the real changes happened inside.

THE END

ABOUT THE AUTHOR

Cardeno C.—CC to friends—is a hopeless romantic who wants to add a lot of happiness and a few *awwws* into a reader's day. Writing is a nice break from real life as a corporate type and volunteer work with gay rights organizations. Cardeno's stories range from sweet to intense, contemporary to paranormal, long to short, but they always include strong relationships and walks into the happily-ever-after sunset.

Email: **cardenoc@gmail.com**

Website: **www.cardenoc.com**

Twitter: **https://twitter.com/cardenoc**

Facebook: **http://www.facebook.com/CardenoC**

Pinterest: **http://www.pinterest.com/cardenoC**

Blog: **http://caferisque.blogspot.com**

OTHER BOOKS BY CARDENO C.

AVAILABLE NOW

He Completes Me
(2nd Edition)

Not even his mother's funeral can convince self-proclaimed party boy Zach Johnson to tone down his snark or think about settling down. He is who he is, and he refuses to change for anyone. When straight-laced, compassionate Aaron Paulson claims he's falling for him, Zach is certain Aaron sees him as another project, one more lost soul for the idealistic Aaron to save. But Zach doesn't need to be fixed and he refuses to be with someone who sees him as broken.

Patience is one of Aaron's many virtues. He has waited years for a man who can share his heart and complete his life and he insists Zach is the one. Pride, fear, and old hurts wither in the wake of Aaron's adoring loyalty and as Zach reevaluates his perceptions of love and family, he finds himself tempted to believe in the impossible: a happily-ever-after.

Just What the Truth Is
(2nd Edition)

People-pleaser Ben Forman has been in the closet so long he has almost convinced himself he is straight, but his denial train gets derailed when hotshot lawyer Micah Trains walks into his life. Micah is brilliant, funny, driven... and he assumes Ben is gay and starts dating him. Finding himself truly happy for the first time, Ben doesn't have the willpower to resist Micah's affection.

When his relationship with Micah heats up, Ben realizes has a problem: his parents won't tolerate a gay son and self-confident Micah isn't the type to hide. If Ben wants to maintain his hold on his happiness, he'll have to decide what's important and own up to the truth of who he is. The trouble is figuring out just what that truth is.

Love at First Sight
(2nd Edition)

The moment naïve, optimistic Jonathan Doyle glimpses a gorgeous blue-eyed stranger from afar, he believes in love at first sight. Unfortunately, he loses sight of the man before they meet and then spends years desperately trying to find him. Just as he is about to give up, Jonathan gets a break and finally encounters David Miller face to face.

Successful, confident David turns Jonathan's previously lonely life into a fairy tale, giving him more than he ever imagined. But the years spent searching were hard on Jonathan, and he's terrified his young son and scandalous past will destroy his blossoming relationship. For David and Jonathan to build a future together, they'll both have to dig deep: David for the courage to share himself in a way he's never considered and Jonathan for the strength to tell the truth.

The One Who Saves Me
(2nd Edition)

At fourteen, Andrew Thompson and Caleb Lakes become best friends. As the years pass, they stand by each other through family trauma, school, and the start of their careers. They share their first sexual experiences, learning and experimenting, and they talk each other through countless dates and breakups.

Decades of trust and loyalty build a deep and abiding friendship, one that surpasses any relationship in their lives. But when the parameters of their unique friendship change, neither man knows how to break out of their established roles to build something new. After all, boyfriends come and go, but best friends are forever.

Where He Ends and I Begin
(2nd Edition)

Aggressive, physical, and brave, Jake Owens is a small town football hero turned big city cop who passes his time with meaningless encounters believing he can't have who he really wants: Nate Richardson, his best friend since before forever. Thoughtful, quiet, and kind, Nate is a brilliant doctor who has always known who he is and has never been able to shake his crush on loyal, courageous, *straight* Jake.

After a passionate night together, Nate realizes Jake isn't as straight as he assumed, but he worries that what they shared was a fluke, a result of too much closeness for too long. For Jake, the question isn't how they ended up in bed together because he has always known that Nate holds his heart, it's how he'll convince Nate that he wants and needs to stay there.

Walk With Me
(2nd Edition)

When Eli Block steps into his parents' living room and sees his childhood crush sitting on the couch, he starts a shameless campaign to seduce the young rabbi. Unfortunately, Seth Cohen barely remembers Eli and he resolutely shuts down all his advances. As a tenuous and then binding friendship forms between the two men, Eli must find a way to move past his unrequited love while still keeping his best friend in his life. Not an easy feat when the same person occupies both roles.

Professional, proper Seth is shocked by Eli's brashness, overt sexuality, and easy defiance of societal norms. But he's also drawn to the happy, funny, light-filled man. As their friendship deepens over the years, Seth watches Eli mature into a man he admires and respects. When Seth finds himself longing for what Eli had so easily offered, he has to decide whether he's willing to veer from his safe life-plan to build a future with Eli.